HOW DO REAL PIGEONS NEST?

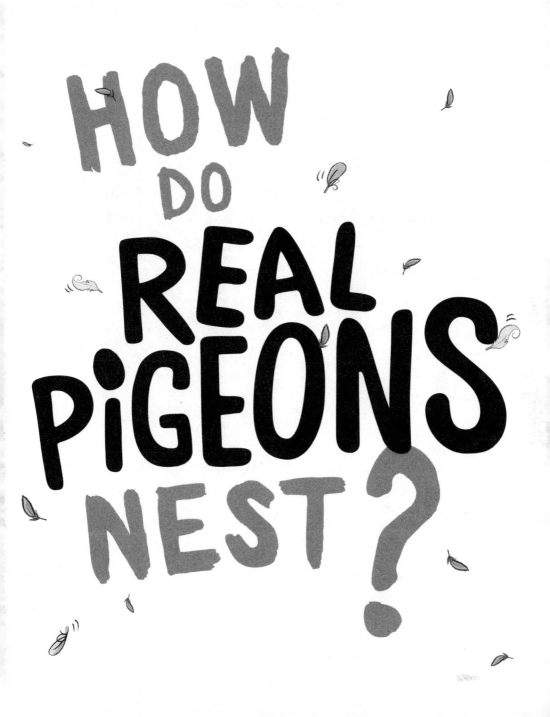

so bendy!

TUMBLER

REAL PIGEONS ALREADY:

- Fight Crime (#1)
- Eat Danger (#2)
And now . . .

HOMEY
directions champ!

ROCK
master of disguise!

REAL PIGEONS

NEST HARD

3

FRILLBACK
superstrong!

RANDOM HOUSE · NEW YORK

ANDREW McDONALD and BEN WOOD

CONTENTS

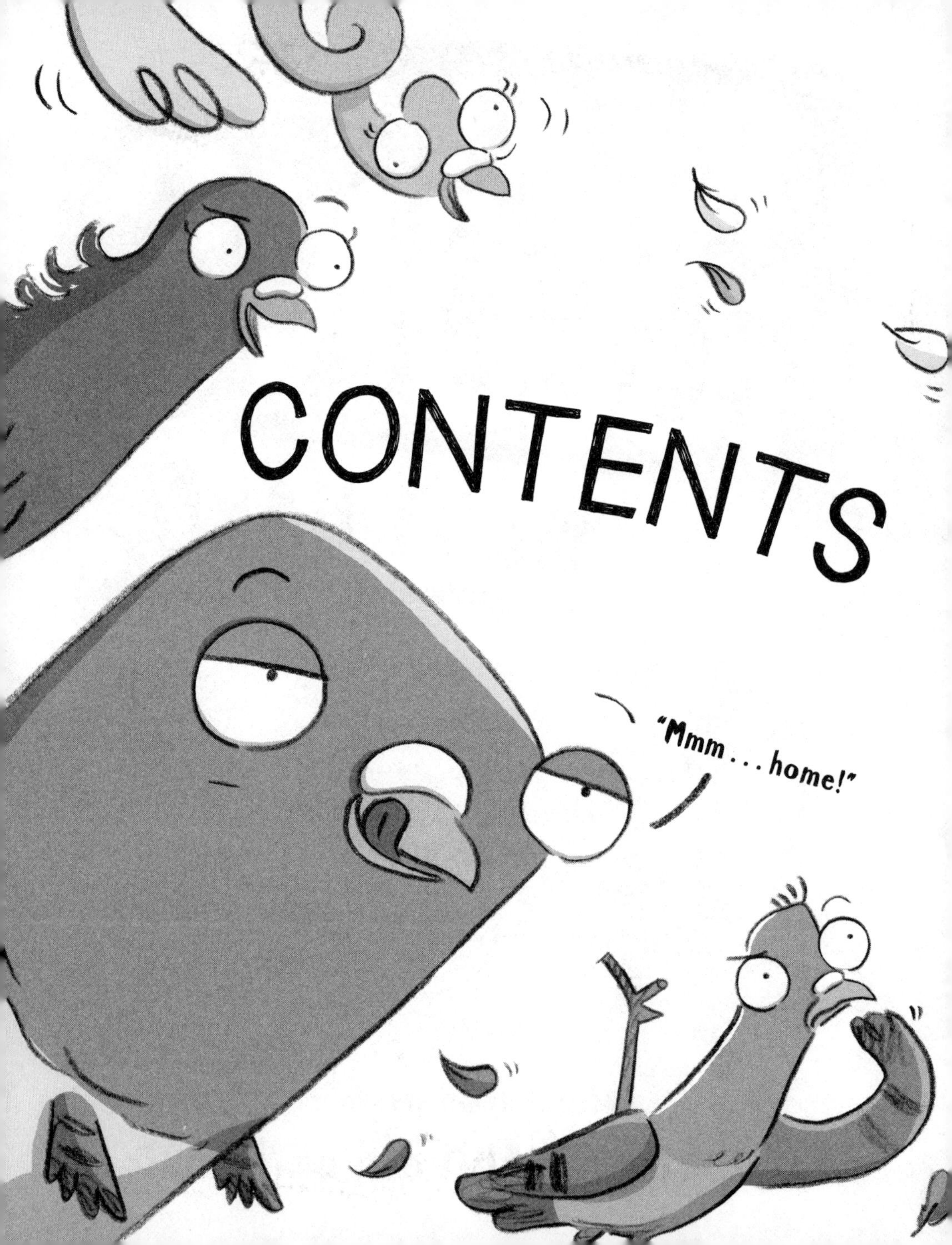
"Mmm . . . home!"

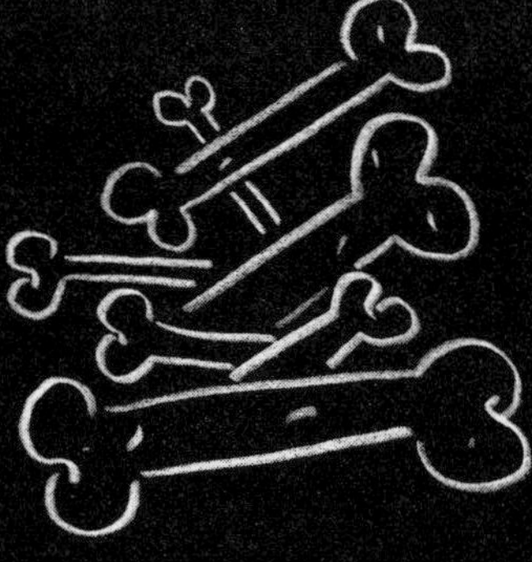

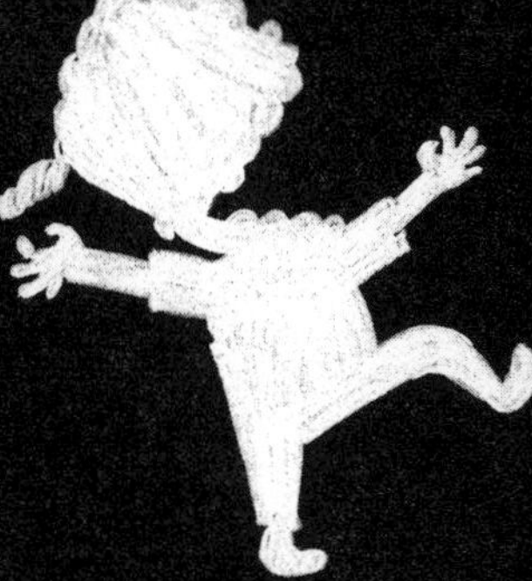

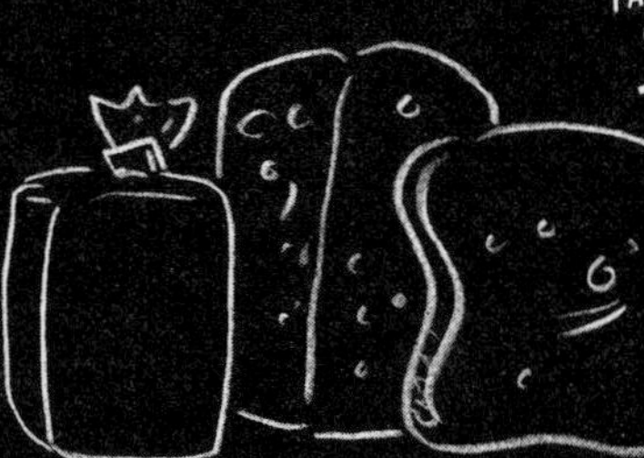

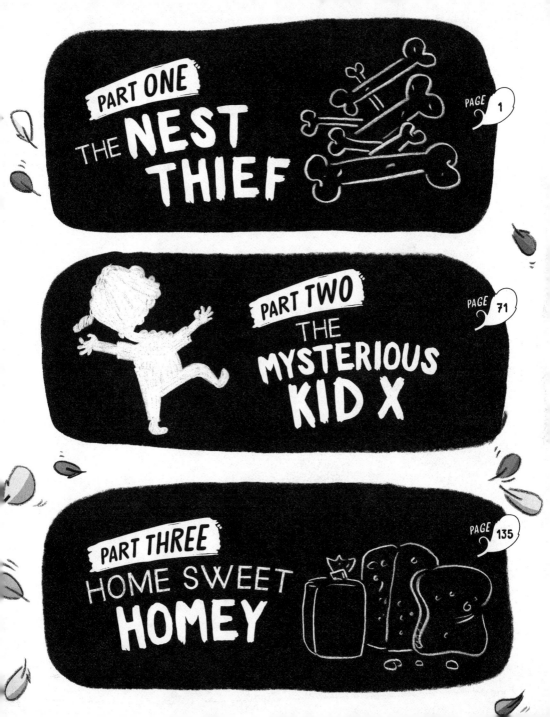

FOR LEIGH McDONALD —ANDREW

FOR JACQUIE, MATT, OLLIE AND ISSY —BEN

Text copyright © 2019 by Andrew McDonald
Cover art and interior illustrations copyright © 2019 by Ben Wood
Series design copyright © 2019 Hardie Grant Egmont

Visit us on the Web! rhcbooks.com

Educators and librarians, for a variety of teaching tools, visit us at
RHTeachersLibrarians.com

Library of Congress Cataloging-in-Publication Data is available upon request.
ISBN 978-0-593-11950-1 (hc) — ISBN 978-0-593-11951-8 (lib. bdg.) —
ISBN 978-0-593-11952-5 (ebook)

Printed in the United States of America

10 9 8 7 6 5 4 3 2 1

First American Edition 2020

PART ONE
THE NEST THIEF

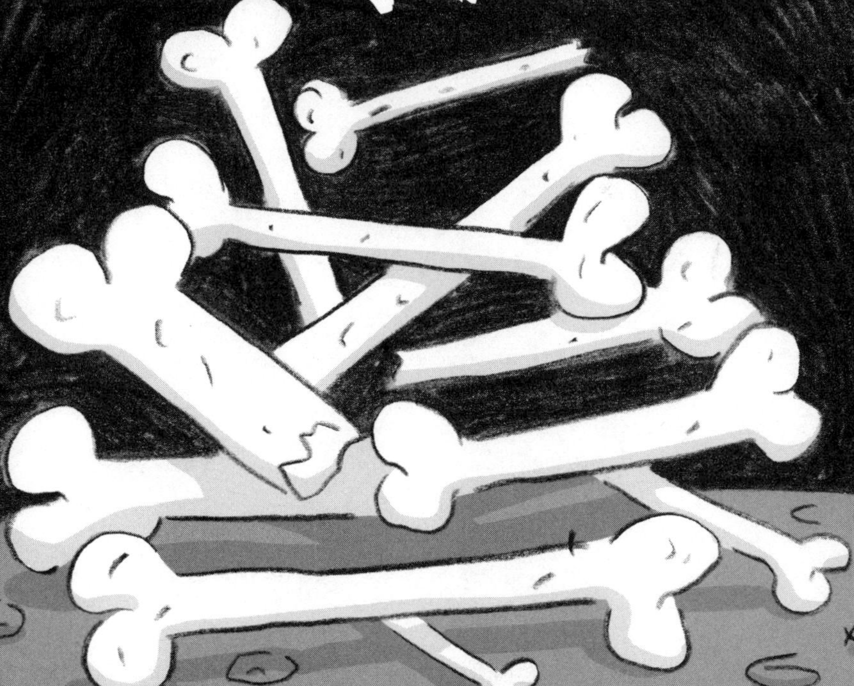

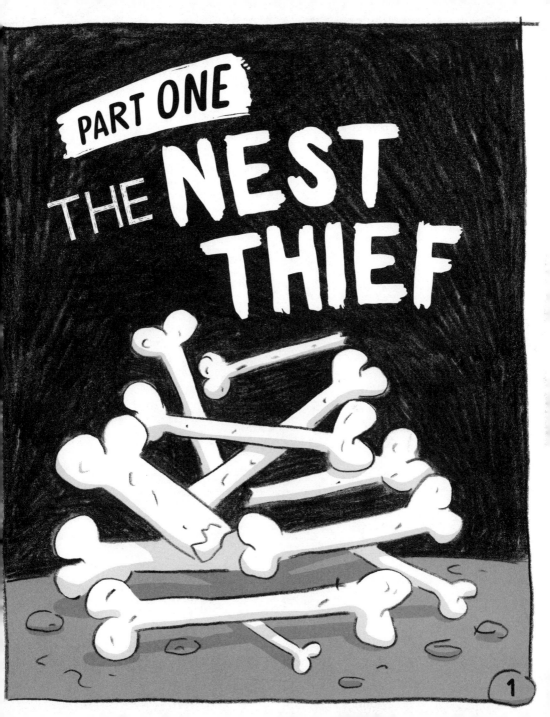

CHAPTER 1

Rock Pigeon is sitting in a shoe.

Is he trying to rest?

Or pretending to be a human ankle?

"It's cold— I should put a sock on!"

Or hoping the shoe turns into a car?

In fact, Rock is in a shoe that's hanging from a power line.

He's waiting for someone.

The entire **REAL PIGEONS** squad is waiting, too.

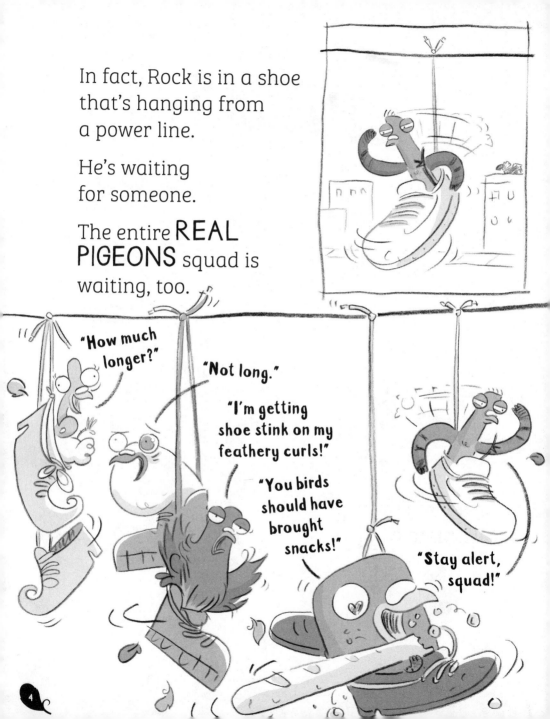

"How much longer?"

"Not long."

"I'm getting shoe stink on my feathery curls!"

"You birds should have brought snacks!"

"Stay alert, squad!"

Finally, a man
walks below them.

Earlier, he stole a puppy! Now it's time for
justice.

The **REAL PIGEONS** get to work.

They chew through the shoelaces holding
them up and . . .

FALL DOWN.

The pigeons do one of their favorite attack moves—FLY KICKS!

FLY KICK

FLY KICK

Rock **BOOTS** the man in the bottom.

Frillback grabs the sack.

The puppy is returned.

The real pigeons **SAVE THE DAY** again.

They go back to their gazebo. But something worse than a puppy stealer is waiting for them.

"HULLO, PIGEONS!"

It's a vulture!

"AHHHHHHHH!"

"He's terrifying and also loud!"

"I've been watching you all," booms the vulture. "You're the REAL PIGEONS, aren't you?"

Rock leaps back in fright.

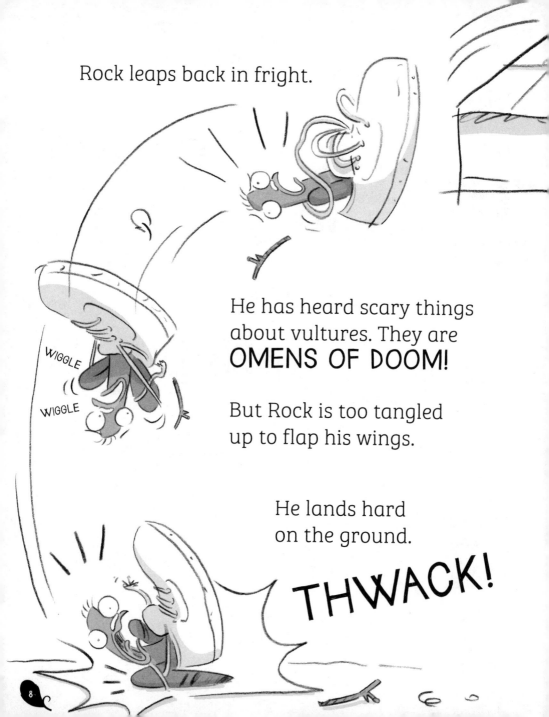

He has heard scary things about vultures. They are **OMENS OF DOOM!**

But Rock is too tangled up to flap his wings.

He lands hard on the ground.

WIGGLE

WIGGLE

THWACK!

Frillback raises her feather fists.

"Stay where you are, **SCARY VULTURE!**"

Rock's wing hurts.

"Ouch!"

"Be brave, **DUDE!**"

Grandpouter bandages it with the help of Trent, Rock's favorite twig. "It's just a sprain," Grandpouter says. "No more costumes for a while, though."

"But being a **MASTER OF DISGUISE** is my **PIGEON POWER!**"

The vulture lands beside them.

"Sorry you had a
WING DING!"
he booms.
**"I'M BEARDY
VULTURE.**
I've been looking
for you because—"

"I know all about vultures!" shouts Rock.
"You are **OMENS OF DOOM.** You must
have **CURSED** me and made me fall!"

"Huh?"

"Don't play dumb," says Grandpouter.
"Everyone knows vultures are scary birds
who **CURSE** and eat **BONES.**"

Beardy Vulture laughs loudly. "It's true. I do love eating bones."

bone broth

bone cotton candy

bone hot dog

"But I'm not here to curse anyone," he adds. "I've come to report a crime. Someone has stolen my nest. Can you **BELIEVE** it?"

Rock raises an eyebrow. "Who would steal a vulture's nest?"

"A HUMAN," says the vulture. "She hiked up to my mountain and stole my nest while I was out for dinner. **SO NAUGHTY!** I followed her back to a house in the city. But I'm too big to sneak inside."

"I want my nest back," adds Beardy Vulture. "I spent ages making it extra-big so I can sleep in it spread-eagle!"

"So will you take the case? **PLEEEEASE?**"

The vulture **SAYS** he's not there to curse the **REAL PIGEONS.** But he still **LOOKS** like a scary bone eater. And Rock's wing really hurts.

If they don't take the case, the vulture might still **CURSE** them. There is only one thing to do.

"REAL PIGEONS FIND STOLEN NESTS...

... SO WE DON'T GET CURSED!"

The vulture starts to lead them to the house where the nest was taken.

"Here's the plan," says Grandpouter on the way. "We get inside, we grab the nest, we get out!"

It sounds simple. But the pigeons have never rescued a **NEST** before. And Rock can't use his **PIGEON POWER.**

They arrive at the house, where there is already a problem. There is a **PARTY!**

JACKIE'S BIRTHDAY BASH

"Welcome to Lady Twitcher's mansion," says a security guard. "Please have your invites ready!"

fancy

fancy

fancy

One pigeon could sneak inside. But a whole squad would freak the humans out.

"We'll have to wear disguises," says Frillback.

"Good luck," says the vulture, flying off. "Don't come back without my nest!"

Some humans wander past with dogs in handbags.

"Hello, **DOGS!**" says Homey. "Why are you in handbags?"

"Because handbags are hammocks that move!"

"Maybe I can disguise myself as a DOG," cries Homey.

He dives into one of the handbags and finds some socks and a stick of eyeliner. His disguise isn't very good, but it will do.

"Woof, doggo!"

The other **REAL PIGEONS** disguise themselves too.

dog

dress

shoelace

wheels

Except for Rock. He feels naked without a disguise of his own. Probably because he **IS** naked. Most pigeons are.

The humans start going inside, and the pigeons move with them. Their disguises are working!

Rock doesn't want to be left out of the mission. He decides to just make a run for it.

Luckily, no one sees him.

"Go, Rock, go!"

When the **REAL PIGEONS** get inside the mansion, they see that someone is greeting the guests.

It's a tall woman in a massive, feathery coat. This must be Lady Twitcher. She looks like she's dressed in chickens.

"Tweet! Tweet!"

says Lady Twitcher.

"**Welcome to the party, tweeties! Come in and see my amazing new . . .**"

And Beardy's stolen nest!

It's huge and awesome and covered in chains . . . and a padlock.

"There's our target, squad!" says Grandpouter. "But how on earth will we steal it back?"

CHAPTER 2

Rock can't stop staring at the nest. It is **AMAZING.** But he is about to get squashed.

So he flies straight into the nearest hiding spot.

Beards are a great place to hide **AND** watch.

"PSST!" Rock whispers.

PSST is a secret pigeon code.
It means: **P**igeons
Should
See
This!

The **REAL PIGEONS** notice
and sneak into the beard too.

All except Homey, who
is enjoying life as a dog.

"I had no idea
bread slices
could be so
thin!"

TISSUES

23

The **REAL PIGEONS** look at the nest.

"Lady Twitcher must want to be a bird," says Rock. "Otherwise, why would she steal a nest? I'll bet she sleeps in it at night."

"Those chains look too strong for me," says Frillback, worried.

"Is there something **IN** the nest?" asks Rock.

Suddenly, a bird flies out of the nest and across the room. She lands on Lady Twitcher's head.

"Why, it's my Jacobin pigeon! Hello, Jackie!"

"WOW!"

"Look at her beautiful feathers!"

The bird is a beautiful **PIGEON** who looks just like Lady Twitcher! How strange.

"TWEET! TWEET! May I have your attention," says Lady Twitcher.

She smiles at Jackie Pigeon.

"Thank you for coming to Jackie's birthday party!" Lady Twitcher says. "I know I'm a bit unusual, throwing a party for my pet bird. But I love her! That's why I got her this beautiful nest as a present."

"It looks so coo!" says Tumbler.

"Vulture nests are rare and expensive," Lady Twitcher continues. "My security guard, Reginald, will keep it safe."

"That's right," says Reginald. "This nest is chained down, and only I have the key!"

Rock gulps. Chains, a padlock, **and** a guard. The nest is going to be **really** hard to steal back.

"If we can't get the nest, the vulture will **CURSE** all of us," says Frillback. "He'll probably straighten out my curls!"

At that moment, all the dogs—and Homey—start to vomit.

"Sorry, DOG PALS! I guess those thin slices weren't bread after all."

little tissue vomits →

"OWWWWW!" says Lady Twitcher.

"I mean ... EWWWW!"

Lady Twitcher looks at Jackie strangely. When she speaks, her voice sounds very pinched.

"Attention, everyone," says Lady Twitcher tightly. "Please put your dogs in the doggy bed. Before they make any more mess. Jackie doesn't like it."

The humans dump their dogs in the big, round doggy bed in the corner. Homey ditches his costume and flies into the beard.

"Why don't I just throw these mutts into the backyard?" growls Reginald.
He picks up the dogs, bed and all.

"Uh . . . no, they can stay," says Lady Twitcher. "We shouldn't be *too* mean to the animals. Should we, Jackie?"

While Reginald is talking to Lady Twitcher, Tumbler makes a move.

"Tumbler!
Where are you going?"

She molds herself into the key shape.

Then she flies back into the beard.

Tumbler is a genius.

She's like a photocopier for keys!

"Now we can unlock that nest padlock with **ME!**" she says, smiling.

"After that, we can pull the chains off," says Rock. "But then what?"

"We could take the nest out through the fireplace," says Frillback. "If it fits!"

"We'll just need to find out where that fireplace leads," says Grandpouter. "There must be a chimney outside!"

"Now we need to get out of this beard without being seen," says Tumbler. "But how?"

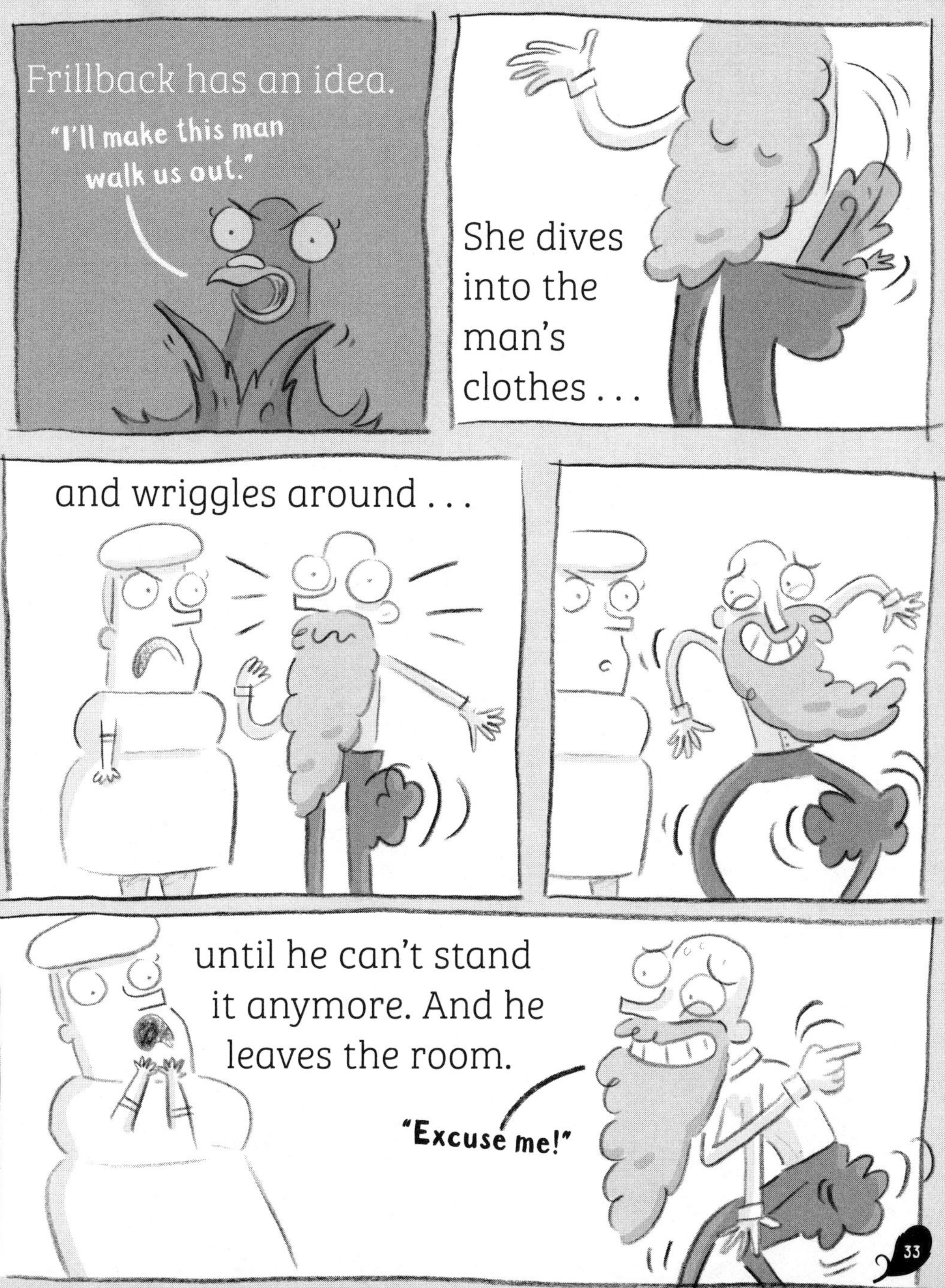
Frillback has an idea.
"I'll make this man walk us out."
She dives into the man's clothes . . .
and wriggles around . . .
until he can't stand it anymore. And he leaves the room.
"Excuse me!"

The man arrives in an empty hallway, and the pigeons fly out.

"Pigeons in my beard? Again?"

The pigeons find a back door.

"Let's go out to find the chimney, PIGS . . . er, I mean PIGeons!" says Homey.

Rock's wing still hurts, so Homey waits with him in the backyard. The others go looking for the right chimney.

"Time for a rest," says Rock.

He flies over to an old grill to perch.

"HULLO?" cries a voice from below.

Rock is so startled he falls off the grill. Is he about to hurt his wing—again?

Luckily, Homey catches Rock this time.

"Gotcha, dude!"

Beardy Vulture is under the lid of the barbecue.

"Sorry to scare you again — I was taking a nap," says Beardy. "You are a little JUMPY, though. Ha ha!"

Rock frowns at Beardy Vulture.

"I can't believe you tried to **CURSE** me again!" he says.

Homey bravely leaps onto the vulture.

"I'm putting you under Homey Arrest!" he says. "For **CURSING** my buddy Rock!"

"Looks like you're hugging me more than arresting me!"

Rock is **mad**.

But it turns out, so is Beardy Vulture.

He stamps his talons. "I have **NEVER CURSED** anyone in my life!" he shouts.

"VULTURES DON'T DO THAT!"

"But . . . you eat bones!" says Rock.

"So do dogs," Beardy Vulture points out. "And they don't do curses."

"Is that a . . . breadstick?"

"No."

"That's true," admits Homey.

38

"Everyone says that we're **OMENS OF DOOM** because we look scary!" explains Beardy. "I'm sick of it. I'm just a vulture with a heart of gold and a good **OUTSIDE VOICE.**"

"Hullo, neighbor!"

"Howdy!"

Beardy picks a sunflower from the garden and gives it to Rock. "I'm sorry about your **WING DING.** But I didn't **CURSE** you. I accidentally scared you, that's all."

Rock thinks the flower is beautiful.

"Thank you, Beardy Vulture."

Rock realizes he has misunderstood Beardy. This vulture might be loud and scary-looking on the outside. But he's SWEET on the inside.

"Does this mean we're friends with Beardy now?" asks Homey.

"Yeah!" says Rock.

"Then it's a good thing I'm already hugging him," says Homey.

Beardy smiles. "Now, listen, I've found a clue. I know where Lady Twitcher lives."

"We **ALL** know that, dude!" says Homey.

Beardy Vulture shakes his head. "No, she doesn't live in the mansion. She lives in that **SHED!** Can you **BELIEVE** it?"

They walk over to the shed.
The door is slightly ajar.

They step inside.

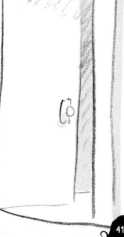

There are books and papers everywhere.

The walls are covered with bird paintings.

Whoever lives here really loves birds.

BIRD BAKERY

"Look! A bakery run by birds," says Homey. "Awesome!"

Rock scratches his chin. Why would Lady Twitcher live out here when she has a huge house?

"Hello, common birds!" says a voice.

It is Lady Twitcher's pet pigeon.

"Hi, Jackie," says Rock, surprised. "We're the **REAL PIGEONS,** and we're here to take back the vulture's stolen nest."

Then Rock looks closer.

"Are those...
moths?"
he asks.

"Yes, my moths carry me places," says Jackie Pigeon. "I am a **QUEEN.** And a true **QUEEN** does not flap her own wings."

"I'm Mith Moth."

"I'm Math Moth."

"You're a queen?" asks Beardy doubtfully.

"Yes!" she sneers. "I **LOOK** like one, don't I?"

"Your Majesty!"

"Don't do that!"

"I thought you were Lady Twitcher's pet," Rock says uneasily.

"I'm not her pet." Jackie laughs. "Lady Twitcher is **MY** pet! I made her throw me this birthday party. I control EVERYTHING she does."

"How?" asks Rock.

Jackie thrusts out her claws. They are **superlong** and **razor sharp**.

"I sit on her head and dig in my claws until she does what I want,"

Jackie says.

"Giving painful pinches is my PIGEON POWER!"

Lady Twitcher isn't a human who thinks she's a bird.

She's just a human under the control of an
EVIL PIGEON!

"Claws are **NOT** for pinching people!" cries Rock. "Claws are for walking. And carrying bread crumbs. And doing **SPIDER SHADOW-PUPPET SHOWS!**"

"Do BONES next!"

"And bread!"

But Jackie smiles. Her eyes are like daggers. "You'll never make shadow puppets again!" she says. "Because I'm going to end you. And stop you from stealing my beautiful nest."

Jackie waves at her moths.

"Fly me to those birds! It's time to get **PINCHED!**"

Rock and Homey shrink back. Jackie might look beautiful, but really she is SCARY and MEAN.

"I'm going to PINCH you to pieces," she sneers.

"Tell her you'll CURSE her, Beardy!" cries Homey.

"Vultures never CURSE. Under any circumstances!" says Beardy.

"We do have other skills, though." Beardy spits a bone toward the wall.

The bone hits a switch, and a light comes on.

The moths suddenly change direction and fly toward the light.

"The beautiful light!"

"I want to eat it!"

"Hey! Wrong way! Where are you going?"

Moths can't resist bright lights.

While Jackie tries to get her moths to turn around, Rock, Homey, and Beardy burst out of the shed and escape.

"Jackie's and Beardy's true natures were hidden," Rock tells Homey. "And that gives me an idea!"

"Does Rock usually sound like he's a few **BONES** short of a **SKELETON?**"

"Don't worry, dude. He is just a deep thinker!"

Rock smiles. Because even though he can't be a **MASTER OF DISGUISE** right now, he's just figured out how to steal back the nest.

Beardy lies low in the barbecue again.

Rock and Homey find the other **REAL PIGEONS.** "The chimney's blocked!" says Tumbler, worried. "What do we do now?"

"Don't worry," says Rock. He explains his plan.

"Jackie Pigeon knows we're trying to steal the nest now! We'll have to be careful."

The other pigeons bob their heads in agreement. Then they all sneak back inside the mansion.

"I'll meet up with you later, team."

Jackie isn't back yet. But they don't have much time. Rock hides behind a plant.

Homey dresses up as a dog again and joins his new friends.

"Hi, DOGGOS! I need a favor."

"Sure thing!"

The mission to get Beardy's nest back is about to start. Rock gives the signal.

"GO!"

cries Rock.

Homey leads the dogs out of the dog bed. They bolt across the room. Straight toward the nest.

BARK BARK

BARK

BARK

THE ROOM GOES CRAZY.

BARK
BARK

BARK

But just before the dogs reach the nest . . .

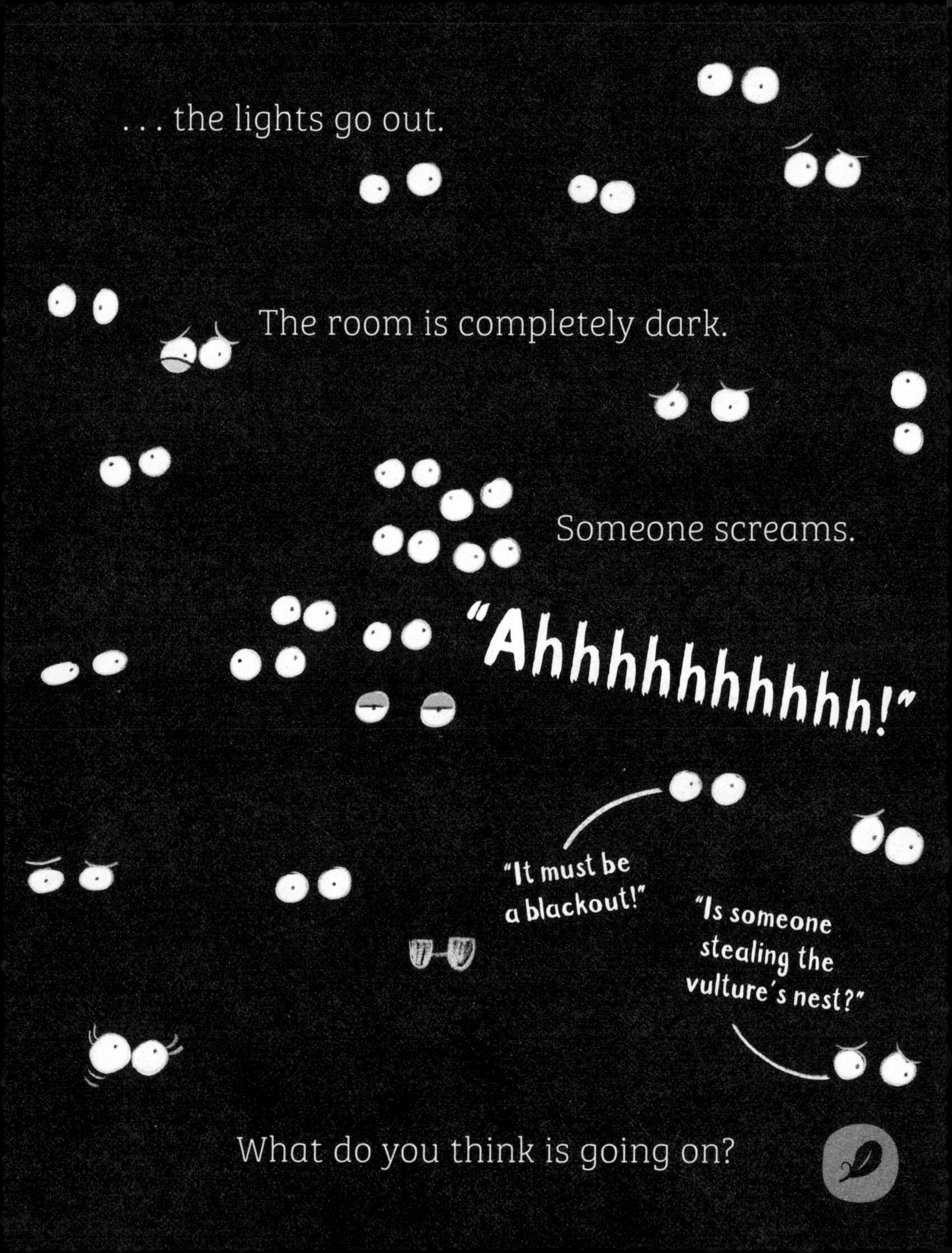
. . . the lights go out.
The room is completely dark.
Someone screams.
"Ahhhhhhhhhhh!"
"It must be a blackout!"
"Is someone stealing the vulture's nest?"
What do you think is going on?

CHAPTER 4

Finally, the backup lights come on. The room is dimmer than before.

Everyone is very confused.

"Good—the nest is still there."

"Sorry I screamed. I'm scared of the dark."

"Keep going!" shouts Rock. "Toward the nest!"

Homey and the dogs start running again.

They're almost at the nest when someone steps in their way.

"**STOP. RIGHT. THERE!**"

It's Lady Twitcher. With Jackie Pigeon perched smugly on her head.

"My beautiful Jackie thinks you're trying to steal her nest," says Lady Twitcher. "What should we do with these naughty dogs, Jackie?"

Jackie Pigeon motions that they should kick the dogs out.

"Throw them out on the street?" says Lady Twitcher, wincing. "That seems a bit mean."

Jackie goes to pinch Lady Twitcher.

"OK, OK," mutters Lady Twitcher. "Whatever you say."

Reginald steps forward. "I've been waiting all day to throw these dogs out!"

Homey and the dogs yelp and jump back onto the bed, barking like mad.

Reginald storms over, picks them up,

marches them outside,

and throws the whole dog bed out into the backyard.

Is Rock's plan ruined?

"Whee!"

OOF!

Rock leaps out from his hiding spot. "I guess you win, Jackie," he says.

The moths fly Jackie across the room. "You again!" she snarls.

"We **tried** to steal the nest back," says Rock, with a funny grin.

"**But you failed!**" cries Jackie. "You **CANNOT** steal a **QUEEN'S NEST**."

"Go and enjoy it, then," says Rock.

"I WILL!" Jackie Pigeon laughs.

She flies up
to the nest.

But she hits
something hard.

Jackie is stunned.

She has flown into a
PAINTING of a nest.

"THE NEST IS GONE!"

she screams.

"Things are not always what they seem," says Rock. "You gave me that idea!"

He explains what happened.

"When I gave the signal, Grandpouter cut the lights. Frillback brought the painting in from the shed.

"I love to EAT DANGER!"

"And Tumbler unlocked the padlock."

Jackie desperately searches the room for the nest. It's nowhere to be found.

"That's it! I'm shaving!"

Finally, she looms over Rock.

"Where is the nest?" she screams. "Tell me or I'll break your other wing, common pigeon."

"You'd better not hurt that pigeon, Jackie!" cries Lady Twitcher. "I'm a bird lover. I won't let any harm come to it!"

Jackie sneers at Rock. "She might be a bird lover. But I'm a **QUEEN.** And **QUEENS** do what they want."

She **PINCHES** Rock **HARD.**

It hurts so much that he falls back . . .

. . . through the air . . .

. . . but doesn't land on the ground.

Because Beardy Vulture catches him!

"Thank you," says Rock.

Beardy smiles. "You're welcome."

Jackie Pigeon flies back to Lady Twitcher. But the human has finally had enough.

"I don't like anyone who hurts birds," Lady Twitcher says. "Reginald—get Jackie Pigeon out of here."

And Jackie is suddenly thrown outside. To live with every other pigeon on the streets.

"This isn't over, common pigeons!" screams Jackie. "I'll get my revenge on you all!"

Lady Twitcher crouches down to Beardy. "You are very brave," she says. "Do you want to come live with me? I love birds, you know!"

The vulture nods happily.

"Living on the top of a mountain can be lonely," Beardy says. "I'll be happier here."

Rock grins.

"Case closed, Trent!" he says.

"Just one thing," says Beardy. "Where IS my nest?"

Rock leads Beardy Vulture out into the backyard.

Where everyone is waiting.

With the dog bed.

Which was used to hide ... **THE NEST!**

"Ta-da!"

"We hid the nest under the rug when the lights were out," explains Rock. "It's safe and sound!"

"Amazing job!"

Lady Twitcher suddenly appears in the doorway.

"I've decided to dress like my new favorite birds — vultures! Now everyone come inside and enjoy the rest of the party!"

Rock might have a sore wing. But the case is solved. And he can still **PARTY HARD!**

THE END ... FOR NOW

UNFORTUNATELY...

JACKIE PIGEON IS ANGRY.

"That was no way
to treat a QUEEN!"
she says. "I'll just have
to start a new KINGDOM."

She flies through
the streets, looking for
someone new to pinch.

"Hedgehogs
hurt to pinch."

"Worms are
pinch-proof
because they're
so small."

"HOW RUDE!"

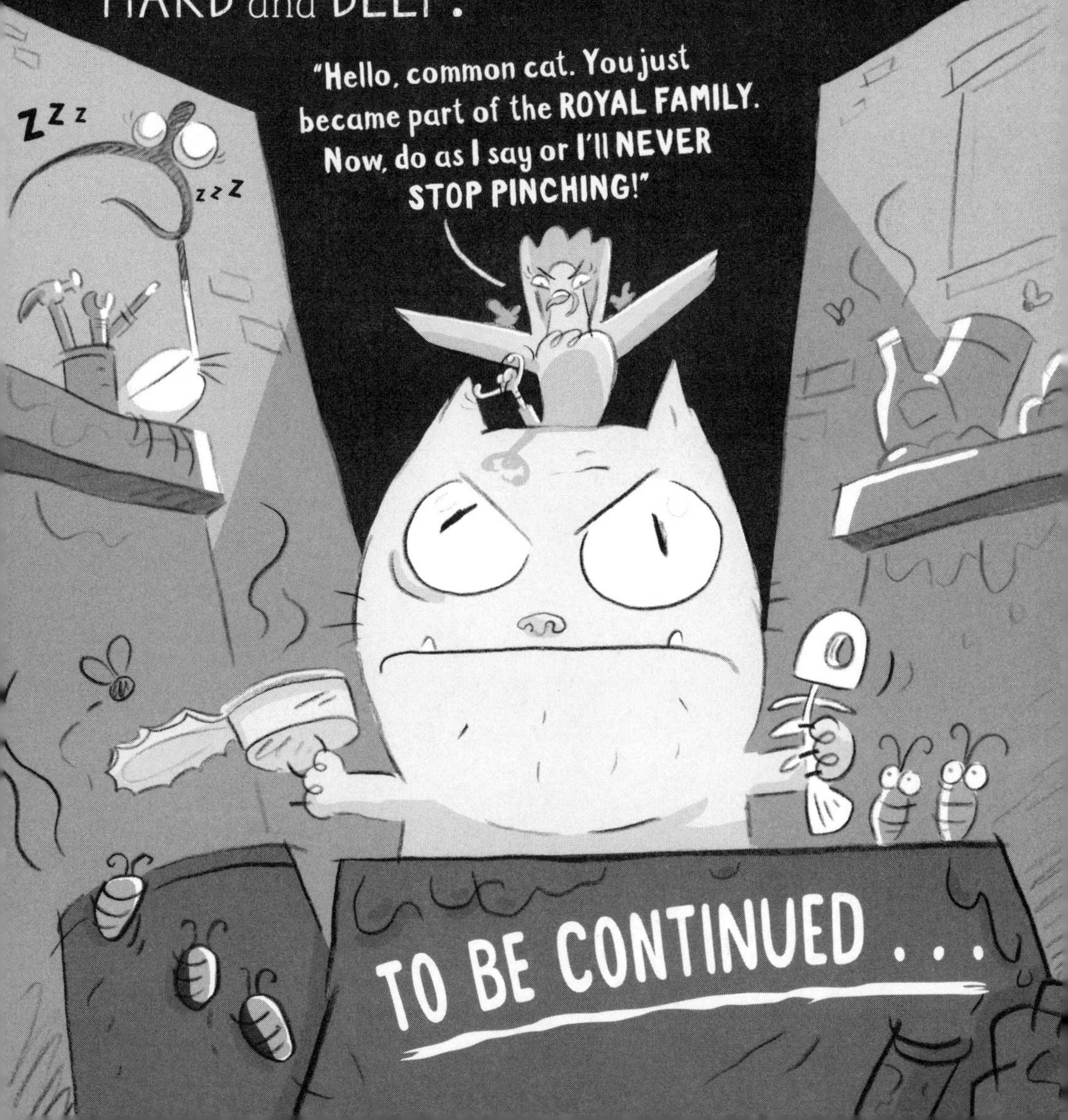

PART TWO THE MYSTERIOUS KID X

CHAPTER 1

The **REAL PIGEONS** are settling down on the roof of their gazebo.

They are going to have a **roost**.

It's just like having a **nap**, but it sounds **WAY COOLER**.

wiggle wiggle

"SNORE!"

"Happy ROOSTING, Trent!" says Rock.

Tumbler usually ties one of her legs to the gazebo. So she doesn't tumble away in her sleep.

But sometimes she forgets.

"Z z z"

And rolls off the roof.

Taking all the sleeping pigeons down with her.

If you have ever woken up in midair, you know how SCARY it is!

The pigeons flap their wings and come to a halt just above the ground.

"Whoops!"

Luckily, Rock's wing is better now.

"That's the third time this week that's happened," says Grandpouter.

"And it's only Monday!" adds Frillback.

"We need to find a better way to **ROOST**," says Rock.

He thinks about his favorite roosting spot when he lived on a farm. He always slept on the head of a llama.

"So comfy!"

"If Rock drools on me, I'm going to head-butt the barnyard wall."

Ever since they rescued Beardy Vulture's amazing nest, Rock has wanted one of his own.

"That's what I'll do," he announces eagerly. "I'll build a special **REAL PIGEONS** nest!"

Rock is awesome at making disguises. But now he wants to be awesome at making other things. **BIGGER** things. Like nests!

So he flies off to find sticks—and some **STRINGY THINGS.**

The **REAL PIGEONS** let him know how they like to roost.

"I want to hang upside down so I don't crush my feathers."

"I like my body all twisty!"

"I like a surface where my CROP will be comfortable."

"I like to dream about bread!"

"You got it!" says Rock.

"The best rest is nest rest."

They visit a nearby basketball court. There are no humans around. But plenty of sticks.

"How do you play basketball?"

"You just pretend the ball is a bird and make it fly."

a stick!

another stick!

so many sticks!

Rock has collected everything he needs when someone yells, **"HEY!"**

"This basketball court is MY home," shouts a peacock who is perched in a tree.

"Go away or suffer the consequences!"

Rock thinks the peacock looks like a turkey who got colored in with blue and green markers. Besides, the basketball court is for **EVERYONE.**

"We're not scared of you," says Rock. "Pigeons are only scared of crows."

"And rain," adds Frillback. "It ruins my curls."

"And DO NOT FEED THE PIGEONS signs," adds Homey.

Rock ignores the peacock.

He puts Trent to one side so his favorite twig doesn't get built into the nest.

He pulls sticks this way . . .

. . . and that way.

He threads **STRINGY THINGS** everywhere . . .

. . . while the **REAL PIGEONS** watch from the sidelines.

When the nest is finished, Rock carries it up to the basketball hoop.

"Ta-da!"

llama-like pillow for Rock

twisty slide for Tumbler

loaf of bread to help Homey dream

built-in crop support for Grandpouter

swing for Frillback to hang upside down from

The pigeons look confused.

Rock has tried to give everyone a spot to roost. But it's a **MESS** of a nest.

"Did I build this right?"

"That isn't a **NEST!**" says the peacock. "It's an **UGLY** hodgepodge of sticks. I'll bet it falls apart any minute now."

Rock has a terrible feeling the peacock is right.

But Frillback defends him.

"Are you looking for a fight, peacock?" cries Frillback. "You shouldn't pick on Rock. Because my feathers are pretty. Pretty **STRONG,** that is!"

The peacock smiles.

"How about a **STARING CONTEST** instead?" he says.

"**You're on!**" says Frillback.

The staring contest begins.

"There's no way I'm going to blink or look away!"

But the peacock has extra eyes.

"Now you are mine!"

Meanwhile, Homey has noticed something in the distance.

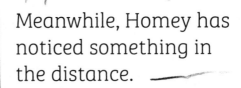

"Don't panic, but there's a **MONSTER** coming this way!"

The pigeons all look over. Frillback immediately loses the staring contest.

"I won! You looked away!"

The **MONSTER** looks upset. Until she sees the pigeons.

Her face brightens, and she runs straight for them.

She isn't a **MONSTER.**

She's an adorable **TINY HUMAN!**

But she's not looking where she's going . . .

. . . and she bangs into the basketball pole.

It shakes, and the nest falls to the ground.

THUD!

CRASH!

"My nest!" cries Rock.

"I don't hate to say I told you so!"

The nest is destroyed. But the TINY HUMAN seems to be OK. And she runs toward the pigeons at full speed.

"PIDGIES!"

THE PIGEONS RUN FOR THEIR LIVES.

The **TINY HUMAN** is closing in.

She laughs and waves her arms like a dancing zombie.

"Why do kids chase birds?" puffs Rock.

"No one knows!" answers Grandpouter. **"It's a mystery."**

The time for running is over. The pigeons fly off, looking for safety.

GRAB
GRAB

Except for Rock, who digs a hole in the dirt.

"Hurry, Trent!!"

He ties a leaf to his foot and jumps in.

He has disguised himself as a **golf hole.**

FLAP FLAP

But the **TINY HUMAN** saw.

She pulls Rock out and wraps her arms around him.

So **THAT'S** why kids always chase pigeons.

"They just want a hug!" wheezes Rock.

Rock looks around. Something is wrong.

There are no other humans in sight.

No humans **AT ALL.** Little kids aren't allowed out without an adult.

So where did this kid come from?

over here?

up here?

under here?

in here?

"Sometimes an **APPEARANCE** is more mysterious than a **DISAPPEARANCE!**" says Rock.

CHAPTER 2

Rock stares at the kid.

The kid stares at Rock.

She is wearing a cute little cape with an X on it. Rock decides to call her **Kid X**. She must be lost.

"Hello, PIDGIE," says **Kid X**, and points to Rock's twig. "What's that?"

"This is Trent," says Rock.

"I like DOLLS! Hello, TWIG DOLL!"

Kid X hugs Trent too.

They are all becoming good friends.

Rock only knows a few things about **TINY HUMANS.**

Like how they ride in fancy cars.

"Nice wheels!"

And sing terrible music.

"WAAH!"

And sometimes have pet bears.

Luckily, **Kid X** doesn't have a bear.

At that moment, the other pigeons reappear.

"PIGS, is it safe to be near a TINY HUMAN?" asks Homey.

"**Kid X** is harmless," says Rock. "But watch out, she is . . ."

". . . a hugger."

"**PIDGIE HUGS!**"

Humans don't actually understand pigeons. But Homey can't help asking **Kid X** a question anyway.

"Where is your family, kid?" he says.

Kid X grins. "PIDGIE, you look like a tiny fridge!"

"FRIDGIE PIDGIE!"

food goes in here . . . . . . and here.

Grandpouter decides to give **Kid X** a quick medical checkup.

"Say 'ahhhhhh.'"

"She's perfectly healthy," says Grandpouter.
"But why she's here by herself is a mystery."

"I wish she hadn't broken my nest," Rock says.
"Maybe I should make a stronger one."

"Don't worry about that," says Homey.
"We have to help **Kid X** find her family first."

Rock knows Homey is right. Heroes always
help others first.

"REAL PIGEONS
HELP LOST KIDS!"

Kid X has a strange look on her face.

"Where **PIDGIE** teeth?" she asks.

"Pigeons don't have teeth," says Rock. "Probably because we'd look **RIDICULOUS.**"

"I think I know someone who can help us," says Grandpouter suddenly.

The pigeons return to the peacock in the tree.

"Come back for a **STARING REMATCH**, have you?!"

"Did you see where this kid came from?" asks Grandpouter.

"No," says the peacock.

But Rock has spotted something else.

"**Look!**"

DO NOT FEED THE PIGEONS

A nasty sign has appeared on the tree.

"Did you put this sign here?" demands Homey.

The peacock grins. "No, I hope you *do* get fed. Because if you can't make a nest, you probably can't feed yourselves either."

"We have to do **SOMETHING** about that sign!" cries Rock.

"Don't worry about it for now, **PIGS**," says Homey. "Getting **Kid X** back to her family is more important."

Bread crumbs are usually all Homey can think about. But not today. Rock is impressed.

All of a sudden, a basketball bounces onto the court.

It's Tumbler! She's wrapped her bendy body around the ball perfectly.

"I found it in the bushes!"

The ball gives Rock an idea.

"If we can bring some other humans here, they'll help **Kid X** get home," he says.

Tumbler bounces out of the basketball court and down the street.

Rock flies alongside her as a guide.

"Keep going straight, then turn left."

"What does 'straight' mean?"

They are looking for humans who can help **Kid X**.

They pass some butterflies.

"Yay!"

"Fun!"

They pass some dogs.

"Is that pigeon controlling a ball with just the power of his mind?"

Finally, Rock sees what they're after—**MIDSIZE HUMANS!**

(Also known as teenagers!)

Tumbler bounces over.

"Hey—that basketball is bouncing by itself!"

"It's a magic basketball!"

"Get it!"

The teenagers chase Tumbler through the streets.

All the way to the basketball court.

But the teenagers don't notice **Kid X**.

Instead they just *play basketball*.

"Man, when I play hoops, it's like nothing else exists!"

"Hey!"

"Lost kid here!"

"Hey!"

pat pat

The plan has failed.

"Bouncing is fun. Being thrown around is not."

And Rock notices something else bad.

DO NOT
FEED THE
PIGEONS

OR ELSE

YOU'RE NOT
THEIR MOTHER

THEY'VE
HAD ENOUGH
ALREADY

"I didn't see who
put them up,"
says Grandpouter.
"But the peacock
didn't move.
It wasn't him."

Rock is worried. He
wonders if Jackie Pigeon
is getting her revenge.
But then again, she's a
pigeon too!

"I am a QUEEN!!!"

"Forget the signs," says Homey.
"**Kid X** is crying!"

"I wanna go home," sobs **Kid X**, wiping away tears. "I'm sick of hiding. A **MONSTER** tried to get me! He had **NO** mouth!"

Rock imagines what this **MONSTER** might look like.

"Help me, Real Pigeons!"

cat head

sharp

no mouth

Kid X isn't just lost. She's running away from a horrible creature.

"We have to get **Kid X** back to her family **NOW**," says Rock. "Before this **MONSTER** finds her!"

Rock uses his **PIGEON POWER** to cheer up **Kid X**.

He dives into a trash can and finds a plastic bag, some bubble gum, and a lollipop wrapper.

Rock Pigeon, **MASTER OF DISGUISE,** has become **Rock Doll.**

wrapper

gum

plastic bag

The tears stop running down **Kid X's** cheeks.

"I love you, pidgie dolly!"

Kid **X** must have run away from the **MONSTER** and ended up at the basketball court.

It's up to the **REAL PIGEONS** to get her home.

"Let's fly around town," says Rock. "There must be other humans who will rescue her."

"Good plan," says Grandpouter. "Frillback, carry **Kid X**!"

Frillback tries to lift her up.

But **Kid X** does **NOT** like being carried. And she throws a tantrum.

"No lift me! NO LIKE IT! PUT ME DOWN!"

They have been grounded.

But luckily, Rock has an idea.

"Come with me, squad," he cries.

Kid **X** refuses to move, so Grandpouter stays behind with her.

Rock leads the others to a supermarket parking lot. He hops onto the handle of a shopping cart.

PARKING LOT
A PARK FOR CARS

"Here we go!" he cries. "We can take **Kid X** around town in this special **KID CAR!**"

Meanwhile, the others are exploring.

Homey watches shoppers go to their cars.

"I don't believe in bags. Food should be carried in stomachs!"

And Tumbler finds a fancy pair of glasses on the ground.

"Someone must have dropped these," says Tumbler. "They make everything look **HUGE!**"

The squad takes the cart back to the basketball court. **Kid X** climbs right in.

"Push me, **PIDGIES**, push me!"

Tumbler looks closely at **Kid X** through her new glasses. She can see three things.

pizza sauce

snot

toothpaste

"It's not unusual for kids to be covered in snot and toothpaste," says Tumbler. "But the pizza sauce looks fresh."

Rock twists **Kid X's** cape around.

"This isn't a cape," he says. "It's a bib! She had it on backward."

"There's a pizza parlor near the supermarket," cries Homey. "**Kid X** must have been eating there with her family before she ran away. Let's go to the pizza parlor, PIGS! This way, Frillback!"

Frillback gets behind the shopping cart, and they push off.

"**Wheeeeeee!**"

As the pigeons leave with **Kid X,** the peacock blows a raspberry.

ppppttt!!

Suddenly, the teenagers notice them.

"Hey, those birds have kidnapped a kid!"

one of them yells.

"Get them!"

Oh no! The teenagers have it all wrong!

They chase the shopping cart across the court.

"You had your chance to save the day!" cries Rock.

Through the park.

"Those **BIG KIDS** are scary!"

And over a bridge.

Until the cart hits a tree root and tips over.

"AAAAAAH!"

CRASH!

The teenagers rush to the crashed shopping cart.

But the pigeons—and **Kid X**—are gone.

"Is that a bubble-gum wig?"

"Huh?"

They're flying for the treetop.

"PUT ME DOWN! NO LIKE IT!"

The **REAL PIGEONS** and **Kid X** sit helplessly in the treetop.

They can't fly away without **Kid X** throwing another tantrum. And any minute now, the teenagers will see them in the tree.

THE REAL PIGEONS ARE TRAPPED!

"When we find those pigeons, I'm going to teach them a lesson!"

CHAPTER 4

"Maybe we should fly off and leave **Kid X** with the teenagers?" asks Rock.

"NO WAY, PIG!" cries Homey. "She's scared of them. We need to get her back to the pizza parlor, to her family!"

"You're right," admits Rock. "Actually, I have a better idea."

He goes back to the basketball court. He collects the sticks from his broken nest.

Rock works quickly. But he isn't fixing the nest to roost in.

"We need a nest that suits crime-fighters," says Rock. "Because **REAL PIGEONS** don't just nest. . . ."

"REAL PIGEONS NEST HARD!"

Rock has built a **NEST PLANE.**

It flies beautifully.

"What a smooth ride!"

"Wheeeeeeeeee!"

"Fly to the pizza parlor!" cries Homey.

Rock looks over the edge of the **NEST PLANE** and sees something shocking.

More mean signs! How did they get onto the plane?

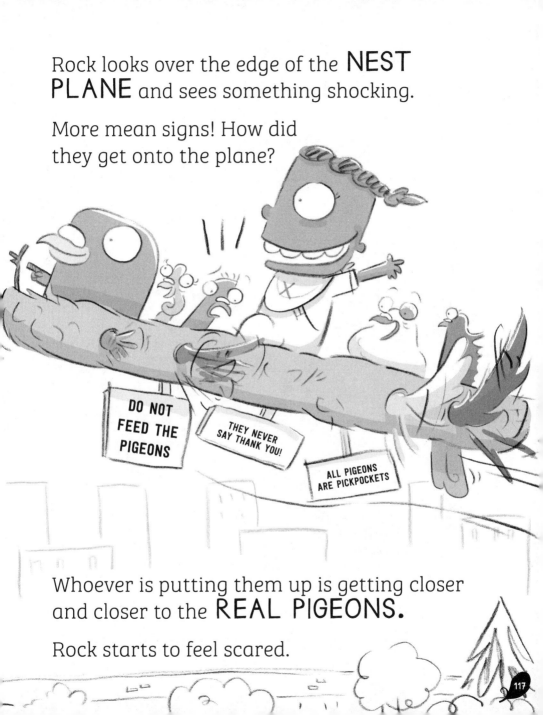

DO NOT FEED THE PIGEONS

THEY NEVER SAY THANK YOU!

ALL PIGEONS ARE PICKPOCKETS

Whoever is putting them up is getting closer and closer to the **REAL PIGEONS.**

Rock starts to feel scared.

The **REAL PIGEONS** have defeated lots of villains. Any of them could be returning for revenge.

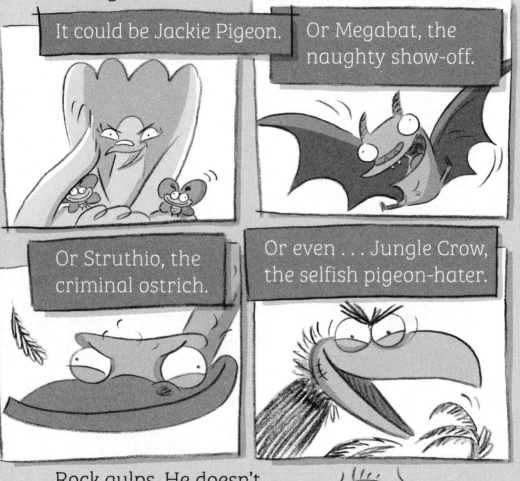

It could be Jackie Pigeon.

Or Megabat, the naughty show-off.

Or Struthio, the criminal ostrich.

Or even . . . Jungle Crow, the selfish pigeon-hater.

Rock gulps. He doesn't like to think about so many villains at once!

Homey aims the **NEST PLANE** at the street below.

The pizza parlor is right there.

"You're almost there, Kid X!"

Rock looks closely. There are no crows, bats, ostriches, or evil pigeons down on the street. But there are humans.

"There are those kidnapping pigeons!"

It's the teenagers. And they've gathered a crowd.

Rock knows they can't just fly down, because the humans will grab them. So he turns to Tumbler.

"Let's try our basketball plan," Rock says. "But do it differently this time. If you know what I mean!"

Tumbler's eyes widen.

She jumps out of the **NEST PLANE** and grabs the basketball from the teenagers.

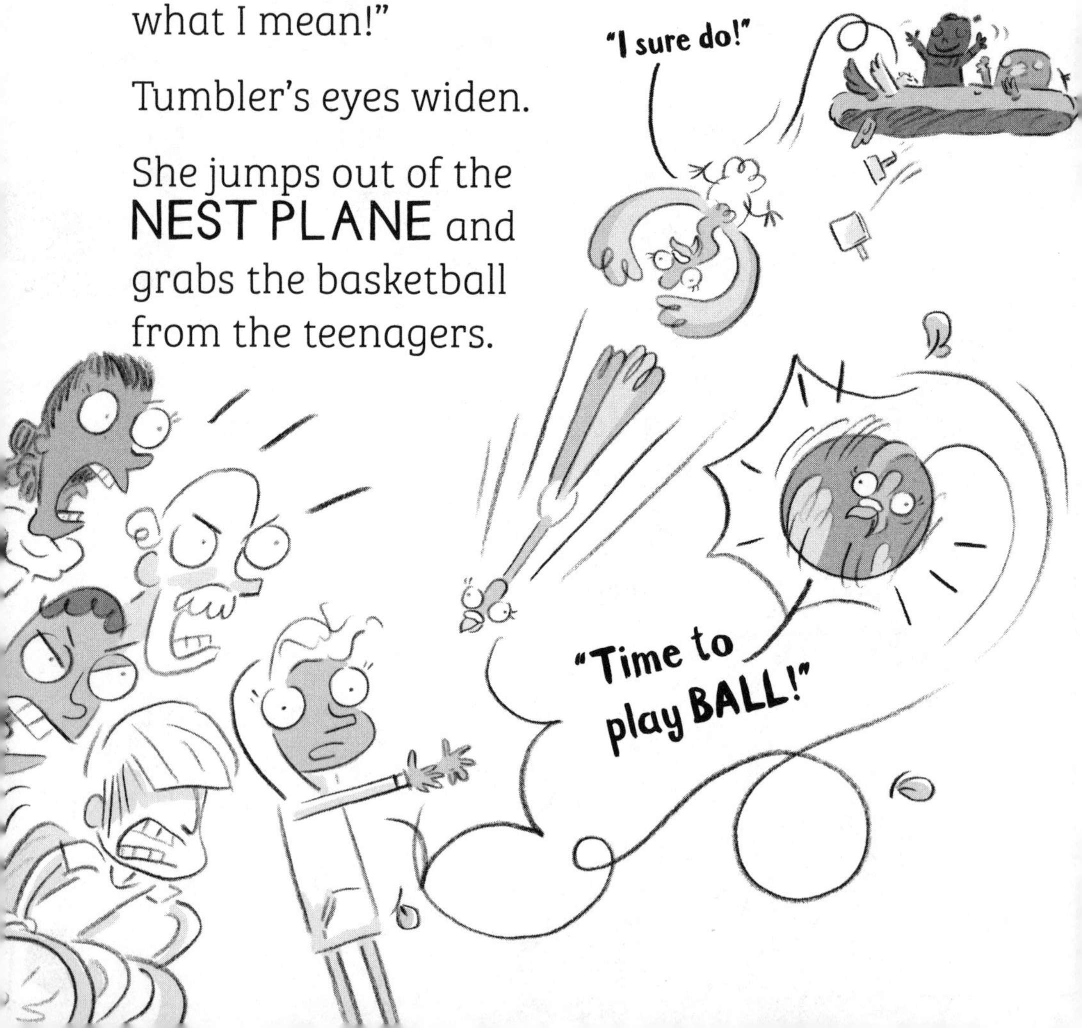
"I sure do!"
"Time to play BALL!"

Tumbler bounces from human to human.

She bounces on people's toes.

She bops heads.

She cannonballs into tummies.

"OW!"

BOP

"BURP!"

The humans scatter.

"Flee!"

"RUN!"

Finally, the **NEST PLANE** lands on the street. But the pizza parlor is **CLOSED**!

CLOSED

They've hit a **dead end.** The pizza trail has gone cold.

DENTIST
X
DR XANADU

"**What now?**" asks Homey.

Rock looks at the office next door, and remembers two important things.

"Where **PIDGIE** teeth?"

"This isn't a cape! It's a bib!"

"Squad, follow me!" he says.

Rock takes them all inside the office next door.

"Oh no!" cries **Kid X** with a tremble. "It's the **MONSTER** with no mouth!"

Except it's not actually a **MONSTER.**

It's a dentist.

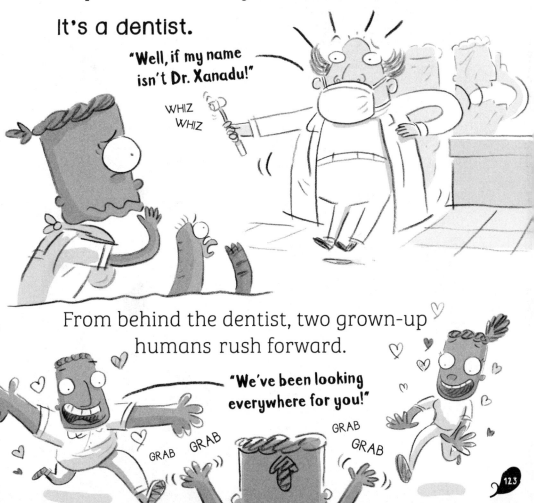

"Well, if my name isn't **Dr. Xanadu!**"

WHIZ WHIZ

From behind the dentist, two grown-up humans rush forward.

"We've been looking everywhere for you!"

GRAB GRAB

GRAB GRAB

The mystery is solved. The pigeons have found **Kid X's** family. Her parents hug her tightly.

Homey is so happy he's in tears.

"I'm just so glad she's back with her family!" he says.

"Is everything OK, Homey?" says Rock.

"I haven't seen my own family in a long time," says Homey, blowing his nose on his feathers. "But I'm glad **Kid X** found hers!"

Rock gives Homey a big hug. Even though he's covered in pigeon snot.

Kid X is still scared of the dentist. And the adults have noticed.

"Those pigeons seem to keep her calm."

"She threw a tantrum when I tried to clean her teeth before."

So the pigeons do one more thing to help Kid X.

They keep her company while the dentist cleans her teeth.

"Almost done."

"I'm brave with PIDGIES here!"

WHIZ

WHIZ

The pigeons say their final farewells.

But Rock hears a banging coming from outside.

"Bye, fridgie pidgie!"

He marches off to investigate.

BANG! BANG!

BANG!

And catches the creature who has been nailing up the bad signs.

IT'S FRILLBACK!

DO

NOT

FEED

PIGEONS

Frillback drops the sign and hammer.

"What are you **DOING?**" cries Rock.

Frillback doesn't answer.
Her beak trembles.
She doesn't seem to
be herself. In fact, she's
been **very** quiet today.

Rock takes a good close look at her.
Her eyes aren't right.

"You've been
HYPNOTIZED!"
Rock gasps.

"Poor
Frillback!"

Rock and the pigeons help Frillback into the
NEST PLANE.

And together, they fly her back to the
basketball court ...

"Excuse me!
Hypnotized pigeon
coming through!"

... where the peacock laughs at them.

"I told you to go away or else," he says.
"You didn't listen. So I hypnotized your friend
during our **STARING CONTEST,** to make
her put up those scary signs."

"You scared me plenty," says Rock. "I thought someone was taking revenge on us!"

"Now please un-hypnotize our friend!" says Grandpouter sternly. "And we'll **ASK** next time we want to visit the basketball court."

"**Fine,**" the peacock says, and clicks his foot.

CLICK!

Frillback shakes her head.

"**I'm so sorry!**" she says. "**I couldn't stop myself from putting up signs.**"

"**You're back!**"

The **REAL PIGEONS** fly their awesome nest back to their gazebo.

"A UFO!"

"RUN FOR YOUR LIVES!"

IT HAS BEEN A
BUSY DAY.

And before they even get out of the
NEST PLANE, they all fall asleep.

It turns out any kind of **NEST** is good for a
ROOST. If Rock were awake, he'd probably
be really proud of himself.

THE END . . . FOR NOW

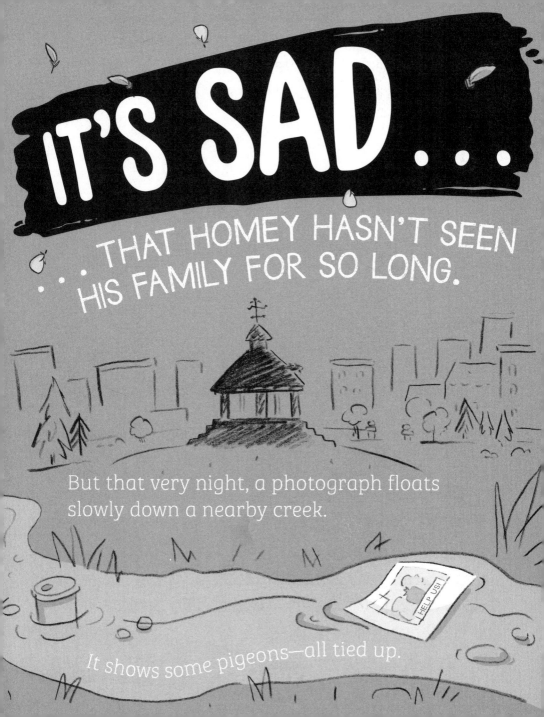

IT'S SAD...

...THAT HOMEY HASN'T SEEN HIS FAMILY FOR SO LONG.

But that very night, a photograph floats slowly down a nearby creek.

It shows some pigeons—all tied up.

HELP US!

They look *very* familiar.

And it looks like they're in trouble!

If only Homey knew . . .

TO BE CONTINUED . . .

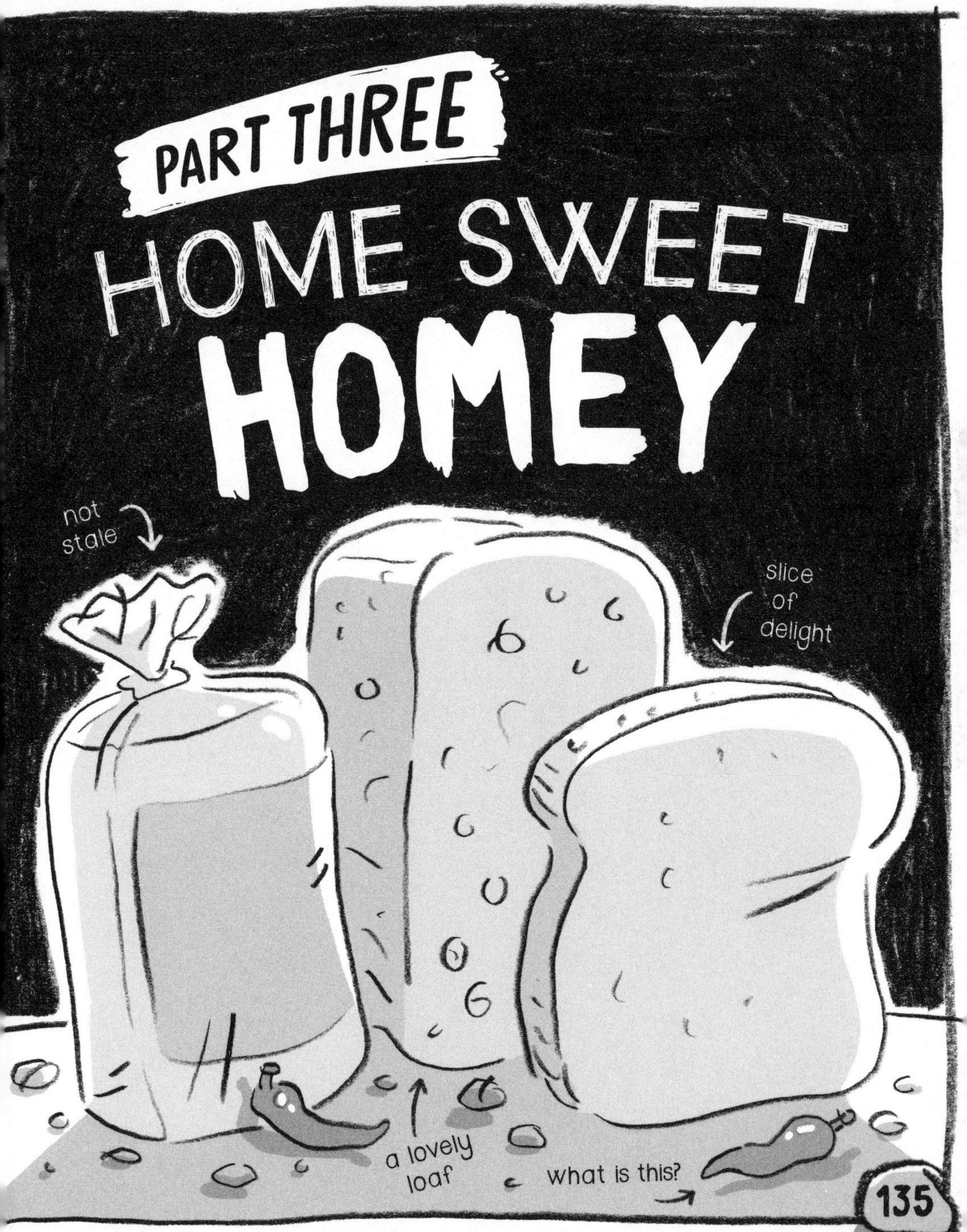
PART THREE
HOME SWEET
HOMEY
not stale
slice of delight
a lovely loaf
what is this?

Rock Pigeon wakes up with a start.

"GASP!"

There is a low rumbling noise nearby.
And it's getting louder.

RUMBLE
RUMBLE

Is there a **MONSTER** coming to get them?

"Can you hear that noise, squad?" says Rock.

RUMBLE
RUMBLE

RUMBLE RUMBLE

But it's not a monster.

The pigeons are just
SUPER hungry.

"RUMBLE RUMBLE
is **TUMMY TALK**
for **FEED ME!"**
says Homey.

No one understands tummies like Homey.

Grandpouter sends the pigeons off to collect some food.

Rock and Frillback collect seeds.

"Ten will be enough."

Tumbler collects raisins.

"Ten will be enough."

Homey collects loaves of bread.

"Will ten be enough?"

The pigeons all bring their food back to the **NEST PLANE.** They are about to dig in to an almighty breakfast . . . when a spoonbill named Bill Spoon drops by.

"Hi, gang!" says Bill. "I found a strange photo at the pond this morning. Thought you might be interested."

Homey takes one look at the photo and drops his bread in shock.

"That's my **FAMILY!**" he cries. "They're in trouble!"

HELP US!

Someone has taken Homey's family hostage!

"Oh no, Homey!" cries Tumbler.

She wraps him in a **BELT HUG**— firm, comfortable, and all the way around.

hug hug

141

"Apparently these photos are everywhere!" says Bill Spoon.

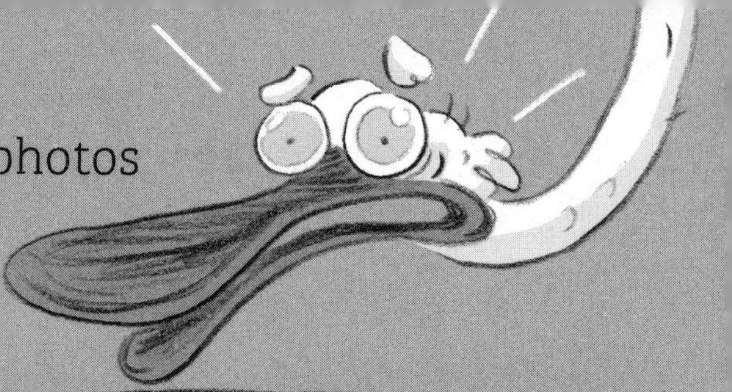

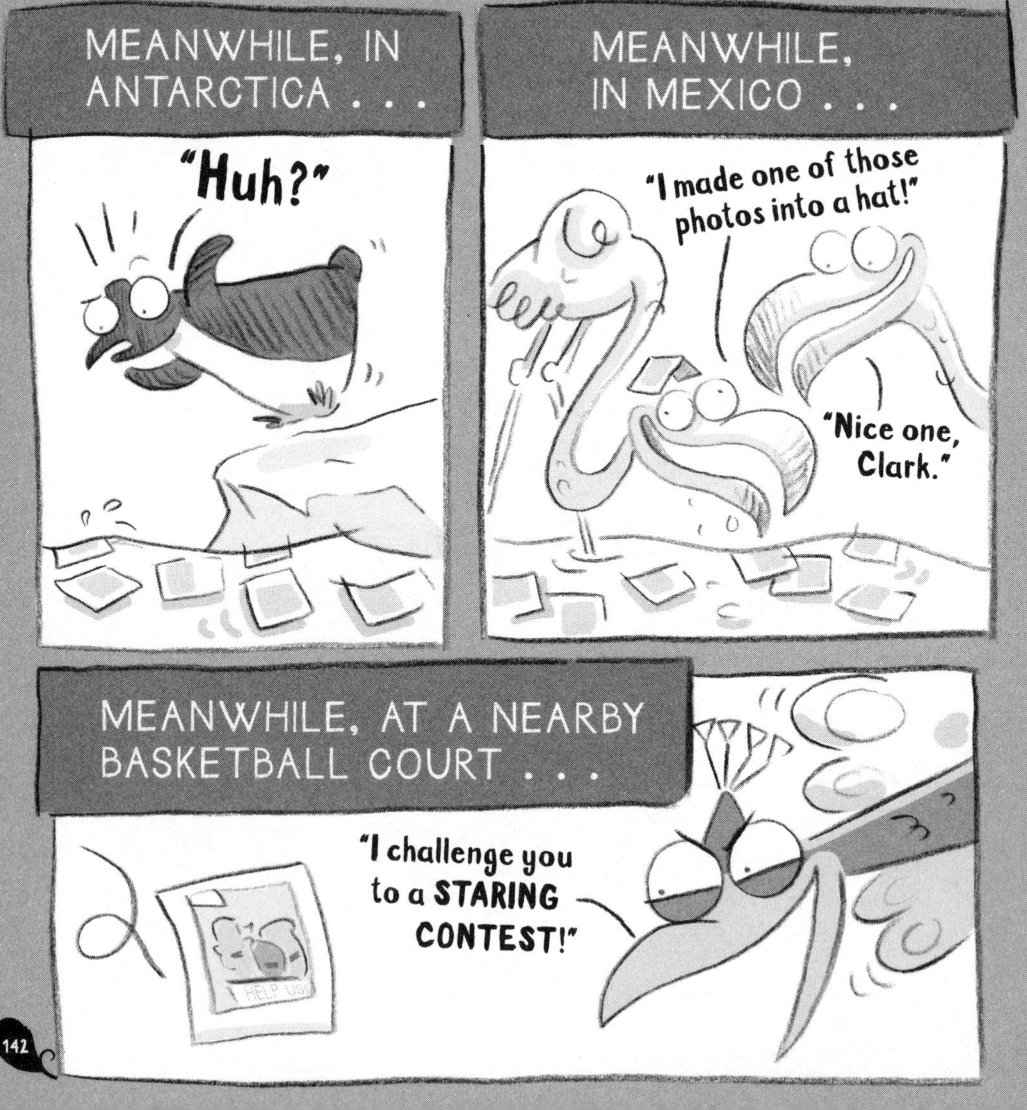
MEANWHILE, IN ANTARCTICA . . .
"Huh?"
MEANWHILE, IN MEXICO . . .
"I made one of those photos into a hat!"
"Nice one, Clark."
MEANWHILE, AT A NEARBY BASKETBALL COURT . . .
"I challenge you to a STARING CONTEST!"
HELP US!

"Thanks, Bill," says Rock. "We'd better go save Homey's family!"

"I'm going to do some **PIDGE-JITSU** on whoever has done this!" cries Frillback.

"REAL PIGEONS RESCUE HOMEY'S FAMILY!"

"It's time to use your **PIGEON POWER** and lead us to your family, Homey!" says Grandpouter.

But Homey doesn't say anything. He just looks at the photo. A single pigeon tear splashes down on it.

"What's the matter?" asks Rock.

"Sorry, **PIGS,**" says Homey. "I have no idea where my family is."

Rock scratches his head with his twig, Trent.

Then he scratches Trent (just in case Trent is itchy).

"But aren't you a **HOMING PIGEON,** Homey?" Rock asks.

Homey sighs. "The truth is, I know how to fly anywhere in the world, except for one place— my family's home."

Homey explains.

"My family are all homing pigeons."

"But I don't remember them much. I last saw them when I was a baby, right before I went flying by myself for the first time."

146

"My homing skills weren't properly developed. And I got lost. I searched for ages, but I never found my way home again."

"I missed my family a lot. So when I found some loaves of bread on the street, I adopted them as my new family."

"Eventually my bread family started going moldy," sighs Homey. "So I ate them. And tried to forget about home."

"So we **CAN'T** rescue your family," says Tumbler, "because we don't know where they are?"

Homey nods.

Rock puts a wing around his friend.

"**REAL PIGEONS** are **REAL FIGHTERS!**" he says. "We'll find a way to save your family. But you can't fight crime on an empty stomach. So let's eat!"

The pigeons all offer Homey their bread to cheer him up.

"Thanks, **PIGS,**" says Homey, taking a bite.

Right away, his eyes fill with water.
He opens his beak to burp.
But fire shoots out.

"FLAME-URRRRRP!"

Rock takes a close look at the bread. "This bread has **chilis** in it!" he cries.

hot chilis!

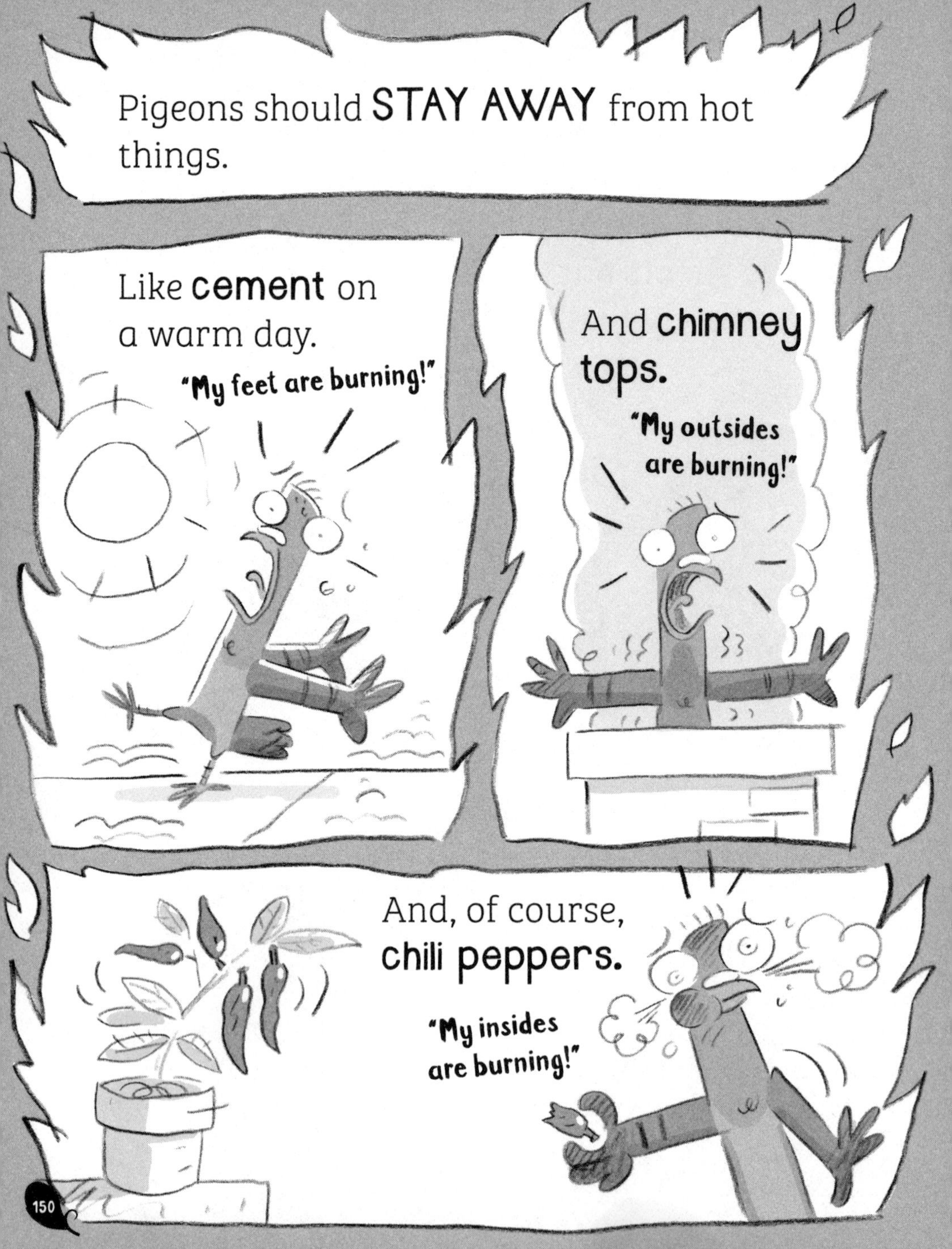
Pigeons should STAY AWAY from hot things.
Like cement on a warm day.
"My feet are burning!"
And chimney tops.
"My outsides are burning!"
And, of course, chili peppers.
"My insides are burning!"

"Who would put chili in bread?" cries Homey.

Before anyone can answer, he sneezes.

"A-COO!"

Chili doesn't just burn.
It can also make you sneeze!

While the others comfort Homey, Rock
notices something interesting in the photo.

HELP US!

"Squad! I think
I've found a clue!"

"There's a mountain with two peaks in the photo," says Rock. "So Homey's family must be close to it."

"I know that mountain," says Homey.

"Come on, squad," cries Rock. "Let's get this rescue mission off the ground!"

"Good luck, pigeons!"

"A-COO!"

CHAPTER 2

The pigeons take off in the NEST PLANE.
Homey sneezes and points the way.

They fly through sunshine.

"A-COO!"

Rain.

"A-COO!"

Migrating geese.

And snow.

"Are you sure we're flying the right way?" asks Frillback after a while.

"No," sighs Homey. "I think sneezing has messed up my sense of direction."

The **REAL PIGEONS** are lost. It's getting late. And they're no closer to finding Homey's family.

"I know where we are," says Rock, looking around.

"That farm looks familiar. Let's make a stop."

"Hoot!"

The pigeons land on a couple of pigs.

"Hey, PIGS! We're on PIGS!"

It's the farm where Rock grew up.
He's excited to pay everyone a visit.

"Hello, everyone," cries Rock. "Guess what—
I'm a crime-fighter now! And I have a twig!
Say hi to Trent!"

"What a show-off!"

"I liked it better when he did wacky costumes."

Homey sees a bread crumb on the ground.

But this bread has chili in it too.

It seems like there is chili bread **EVERYWHERE.**

Grandpouter takes Homey to visit some cows. "Milk helps wash that chili taste away!" he explains.

"Thanks, cows!" cries Homey.

"How unusual."

"Time to go again!" Homey yawns. "We have to be **RESCUE PIGEONS!**"

But Grandpouter shakes his head. "It's very late," he says. "I know you're worried about your family, but let's get some sleep. We'll head off first thing in the morning."

Rock takes them to the llamas.

"This used to be my favorite sleeping spot. Llamas are even comfier than nests!"

The pigeons wrap themselves in llama ears and fall asleep.

The next morning, just as the sun is rising, a rooster throws back its head to crow.

But its head comes off.

"Cock-a-doodle . . .

. . . whoops!"

"We missed you, weird pigeon!"

Now it's time for the REAL PIGEONS to find Homey's family.

"Bye, everyone!"

"I can't believe they slept on us when they had a perfectly good nest."

"Typical."

Homey is feeling much better today. He guides the pigeons over valleys and small towns.

Until they finally reach the mountain with two peaks. And they see something amazing.

BUTTERWORTH BIRD BAKERY **THIS WAY** ➡

"**Wow!**"

Homey's family is on a giant billboard.

"Homey, it looks like your family are ... BAKERS!" says Rock.

Homey is overjoyed.

"No wonder I love bread so much!" he cries.

"Makes perfect sense!"

"We should check the bakery for clues," says Rock.

The pigeons arrive at the bakery and park the **NEST PLANE.**

"This place looks familiar."

But it's obvious that things are **NOT RIGHT.**

MEGABREAD

Because there is a different sign on the building.

A pack of **CATS** runs out of the bakery, hissing and snorting.

HISS HISS

SNORT

And standing on the head of the biggest cat . . .

PINCH PINCH

. . . is Jackie, **THE EVIL PIGEON!**

The **REAL PIGEONS** shiver in the tree.

Jackie Pigeon was already dangerous. But now that she is controlling a **CAT PACK** with her claws, she is an even bigger threat!

"I am **QUEEN** of the **CATS,**" Jackie cries. "Now, don't make me get pinchy! Get to work!"

The cats run off into the distance.

Jackie hovers in the air. "Take me back into the bakery!" she growls at her moths.

What is Jackie Pigeon doing here?

"Has she taken my family hostage?" wails Homey.

"Maybe she is getting revenge on us!" says Rock.

Rock only knows one thing for sure.

"We **HAVE** to get inside that bakery!" he cries. "But we'll need disguises so that Jackie doesn't recognize us."

"I'm sure we can think up good disguises if we put our heads together," says Tumbler.

"And maybe our bodies too," says Rock. "That gives me an idea!"

Rock explains his plan.
The **REAL PIGEONS** huddle together.
And get all tangled up.

Until they are in position.

And look just like . . .

Since Rock is the **MASTER OF DISGUISE,**
he explains **HOW TO BE AN OWL.**

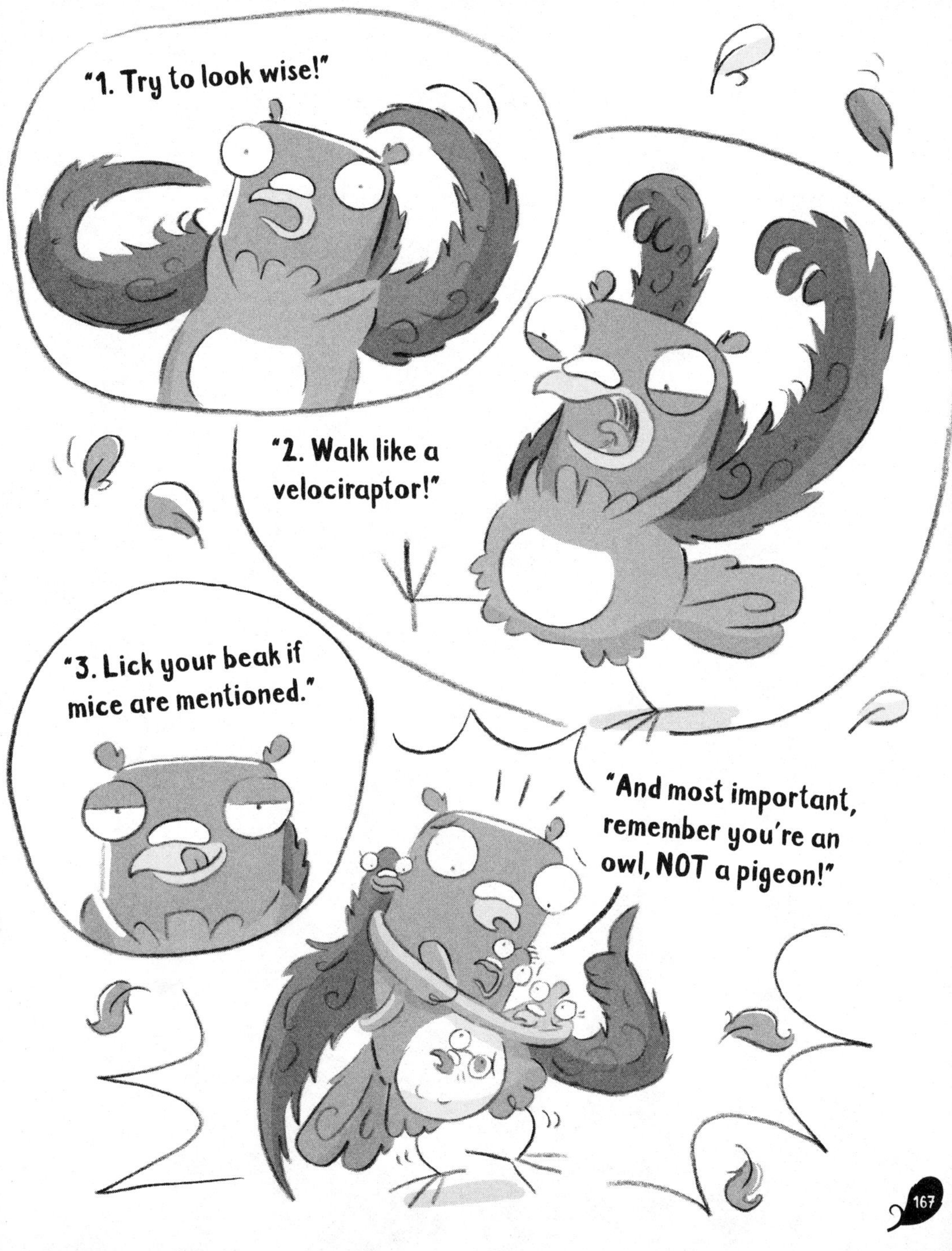
"1. Try to look wise!"
"2. Walk like a velociraptor!"
"3. Lick your beak if mice are mentioned."
"And most important, remember you're an owl, NOT a pigeon!"

They walk into the bakery and are shocked to see four very familiar faces.

JUNGLE CROW!

STRUTHIO OSTRICH!

MEGABAT!

AND JACKIE PIGEON TOO!

Why are all these villains here?

CHAPTER 3

"Welcome to our bakery," says Jungle Crow. "Who are you?"

Homey is the head of the owl. Which means he needs to talk. But being close to so many villains has made him nervous!

"OWL!" he says suddenly. **"NOT A PIGEON!"**

Has Homey given the squad away?

"Al Notapigeon?
That's a weird name,"
says Jungle Crow.
But then he smiles.
"It's nice to meet you, **Al**."

The villains have taken over the bakery!
Homey's family must be in here somewhere.

But why would villains want to make *bread*?
They could be doing **MUCH** more evil things.

Homey clears his throat.

"Could I have a tour?
Then I will eat some
bread. Or a mouse.
Or some mouse bread."

"A tour?" says Jungle Crow.

"Just do it," says Jackie.

"Don't tell me what to do!"

"The more people who know about our bread, the better," Megabat says.

"HURRY UP," orders Struthio Ostrich. "TOUR TIME!"

"OK, OK," says Jungle Crow. "Follow me, AI." They go to the back of the bakery.

"This is where we make our **MEGABREAD!**" says Jungle Crow. "It's a new kind of bread. Struthio Ostrich kneads the dough with his head."

"**HEAD STRONG,**" says Struthio. "**BREAD BONK!**"

"That's a giant ball of dough!"

"I love dough! It's basically baby bread!"

"I work the oven," says Jungle Crow.

"Megabat is our mascot," Jungle Crow explains. "He puts labels on the loaves."

"Megabread will make me the most famous bat in the world."

"And Jackie Pigeon sends the bread out into the world."

"My cats are a great delivery service," says Jackie.

Homey normally loves bread-talk. But right now he just wants to find his family.

"Before we go on, I need to get these loaves out of the oven, Al," says Jungle Crow.

"This is our chance," whispers Rock. "Let's go look for Homey's family."

"Great tour," says Homey.

"But I think I saw a mouse outside. Gotta go, dudes!"

The pigeons pretend to leave the bakery. But as soon as they're out of sight, they separate to search for the kidnapped bakers.

Tumbler looks in the cupboards.

Grandpouter searches in the flour.

COUGH COUGH

Frillback checks the freezer.

Rock and Homey hear scratching noises coming from behind a door.

They dart in to find . . .

... a room packed full of **junk.**

With three pigeons tied up in the corner, taking a selfie with an old Polaroid camera.

It's Homey's family!

Homey and Rock untie the hostages.
The trio leaps on Homey in joy.

"FAMILY PIGS!"
cries Homey.

"Homey??"

"Brother!"

"Where did you go?
We thought we'd
lost you forever!"

He has finally found his family!

"We found one of your photos!" Homey says.

"I knew that if we kept slipping them out the window, someone would rescue us," says his dad, Homer. "But I never dreamed our rescuer would be you, Homestead Butterworth!"

"Who is **Homestead Butterworth?**" asks Rock.

"That's Homey!" says his mom. "'Homey' is short for 'Homestead.'"

Yet this is no time for a reunion. Rock tries to open the window, but it's rusted in place.

"Pull, Trent!"

"We need to get out of here," he says. "Before those villains discover us."

"Let's use our PIGEON POWERS!" says Homey's family.

179

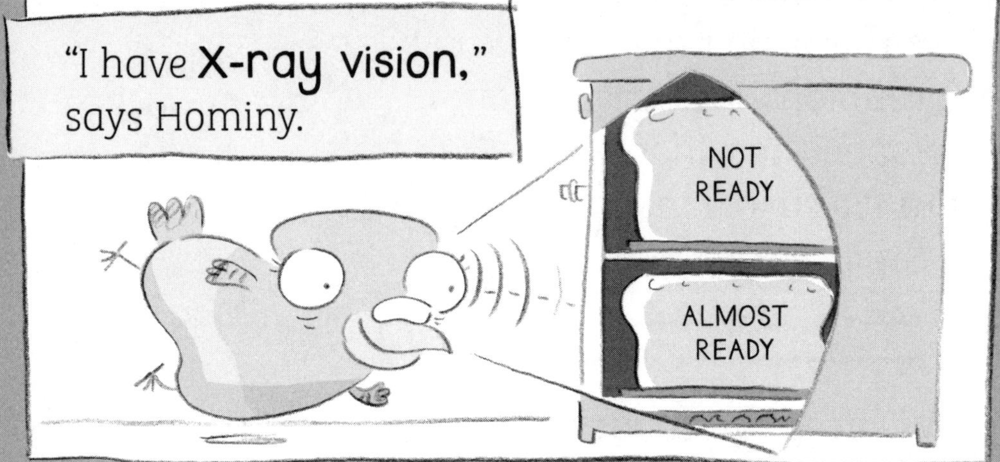
"I have **X-ray vision,"** says Hominy.
NOT READY
ALMOST READY

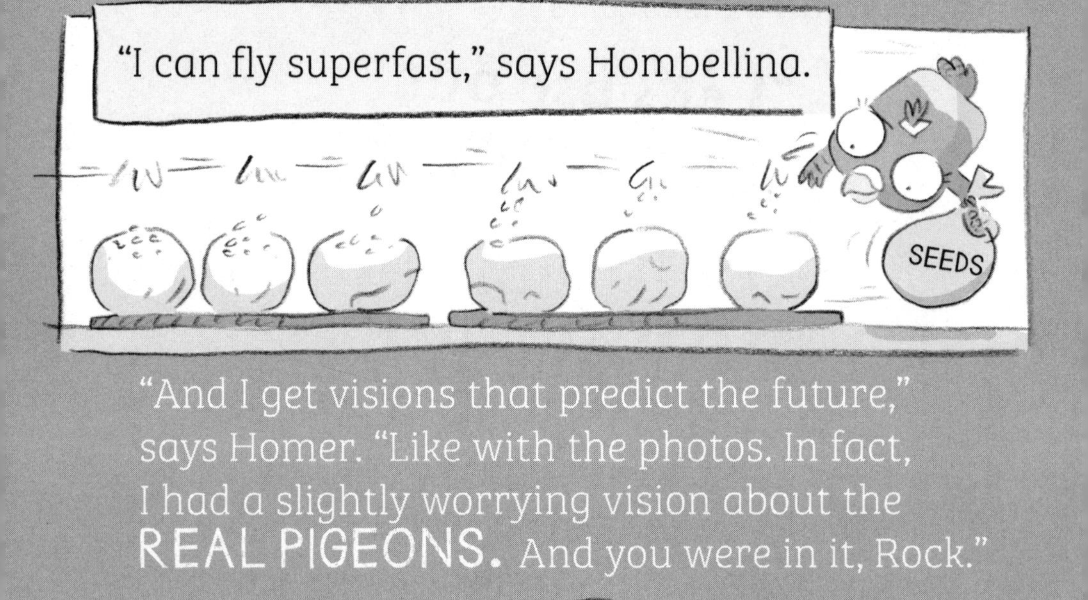
"I can fly superfast," says Hombellina.
SEEDS

"And I get visions that predict the future," says Homer. "Like with the photos. In fact, I had a slightly worrying vision about the **REAL PIGEONS.** And you were in it, Rock."

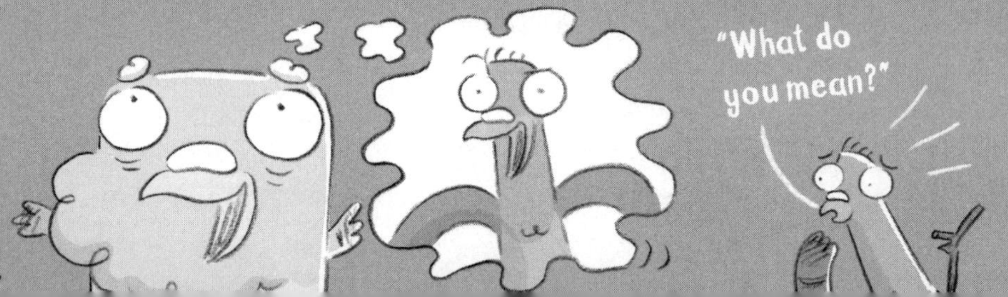
"What do you mean?"

But before Homer can explain, the other pigeons burst into the room.

The pigeons become Al Notapigeon again just as the villains appear.

But Homey has forgotten the feathers that look like ears.

Struthio steps forward. **"NICE COSTUME— FAKE OWL!"**

"Hoot?"

He kicks Al Notapigeon in the tummy, and the pigeons separate.

THEY HAVE BEEN EXPOSED!

CHAPTER 4

"So **AI Notapigeon** actually is **pigeons**," sneers Jungle Crow. "Your time is UP, REAL PIGEONS!"

PINCH

PINCH

Jackie's cats crawl into the room.

The pigeons are **COMPLETELY** surrounded by danger.

Jungle Crow breaks a breadstick in half and tosses it into his beak.

Jungle Crow is bad. But Rock doesn't want him to suffer.

"Don't eat that!" cries Rock. "It's **chili bread!**"

"I KNOW," laughs Jungle Crow, swallowing. "Megabread is **chili bread.** Crows can eat chili without a problem. But pigeons can't—ha ha!"

Jungle Crow used to be behind bars, but he explains that he and Megabat escaped their cage.

And started an **ANTI-PIGEON CLUB.**

ANTI-PIGEON CLUB.

FIRST MEETING THIS TUESDAY

BRING A PLATE OF FOOD

Struthio escaped his ostrich farm to join the club.

And Jackie couldn't resist either.

"Our revenge was making bread *you* can't eat!" cries Jungle Crow.

So *that's* why the villains have taken over Homey's family's bakery.

"I'm also here hoping to get famous," adds Megabat.

Jackie leans forward, her eyes glowing with madness. "But now our revenge will be final. I'll feed you to my cats!"

IS THIS THE END FOR THE REAL PIGEONS SQUAD?

"ENOUGH!" cries Homey. "You've taken over this bakery. You've tied up my family. And you've even RUINED BREAD.

STOP IT NOW!"

"Or what?" laughs Jungle Crow. "You'll give me bad directions? You're a **homing pigeon.** What can you possibly do to scare me?"

Homey grins. **"I can EAT!"**

He shoves ten loaves of **chili bread** into his beak.

"Here we go!"

Homey's eyes water.

Smoke pours out
of his ears.

He opens his beak and . . .

"FLAME

―URRRRRP!"

Homey breathes fire at the villains and the cats. It's total chaos!

"My brother is a fire-breather!"

The other pigeons escape!

But then Homey runs out of fire breath.

The villains turn back. "Get him!" Jungle Crow cries.

RUMBLE RUMBLE

"What's that rumbling noise?"

"It's not a tummy this time!"

A giant ball of bread dough rolls into the room. It's **PIGEONS** to the rescue!

RUMBLE

RUMBLE

The dough collects all the villains . . .

. . . and **SMASHES** through the wall to the outside.

"What should we do with all these villains and cats?" asks Rock.

"Get them out of my sight!" says Homey.

"A-COO!"

"I can do that," says Frillback.

And she kicks the ball high into the sky.

"NOOOOOOOOOOOOO!"

Homey thrusts a wing in the air.

"I declare the era of **chili bread OVER!**" he says. "Now my family can be bakers again!"

THE PIGEONS ALL CHEER.

"Good kick!"

"Hooray!" cries Rock. "Now let's go home, Homey."

But Homey shakes his head. "I'm sorry, **PIGS.** I want to stay with my family and learn how to be a baker. But that means I'll have to quit the **REAL PIGEONS** squad."

The REAL PIGEONS start to tear up.

"Homey!
Nooooo!"
"What?!"
"We can't be
PIGS without you!"
"How will we
find our way
home?!"

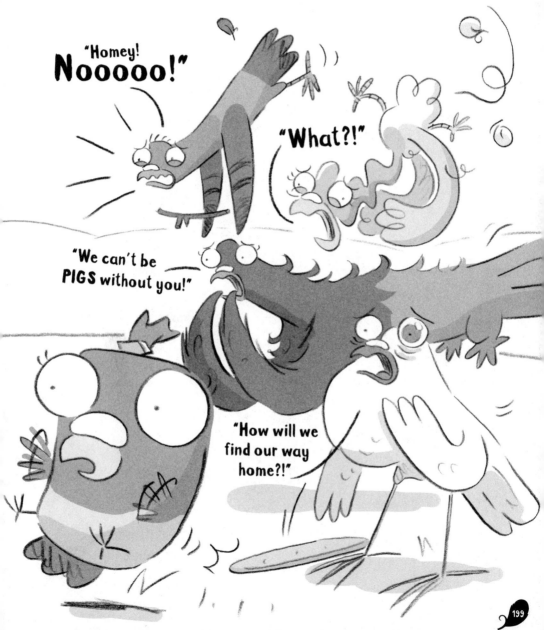

But then Hombellina has an idea.

"Why don't you all spend the summer here? We'll teach Homey how to bake. And after that you can fight crime again!"

"Great idea, little **PIG**," says Homey.

"Did my brother just call me a **PIG**?" says Hombellina.

"Still happy he found you?" Frillback winks.

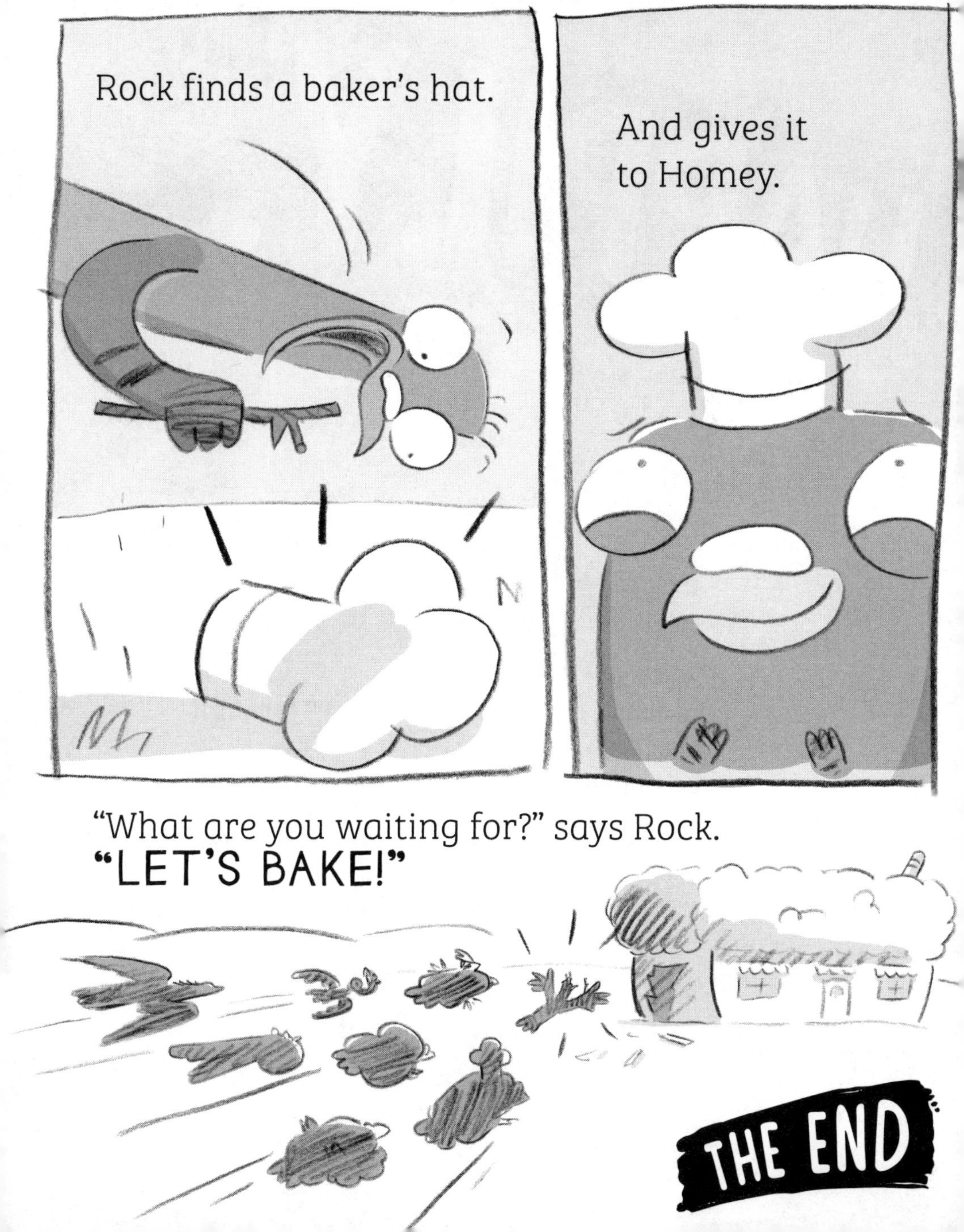
Rock finds a baker's hat.
And gives it to Homey.
"What are you waiting for?" says Rock.
"LET'S BAKE!"
THE END

HAPPILY...

THE REAL PIGEONS ENJOY THEIR SUMMER.

Homey learns all the family secrets.

Tumbler and Hombellina become friends.

"Woocoo!"

And they have a big **chili** bonfire.

But something is still bothering Rock.

So he finds Homey's dad.

"You said you had an upsetting vision about the squad, Homer," Rock says. "What did you see?"

Homer sighs. "You're not going to like it."

But Rock needs to know.

"Please tell me!"

"Very well," says Homer. "The REAL PIGEONS squad will END, and it will END soon!"

"GASP!"

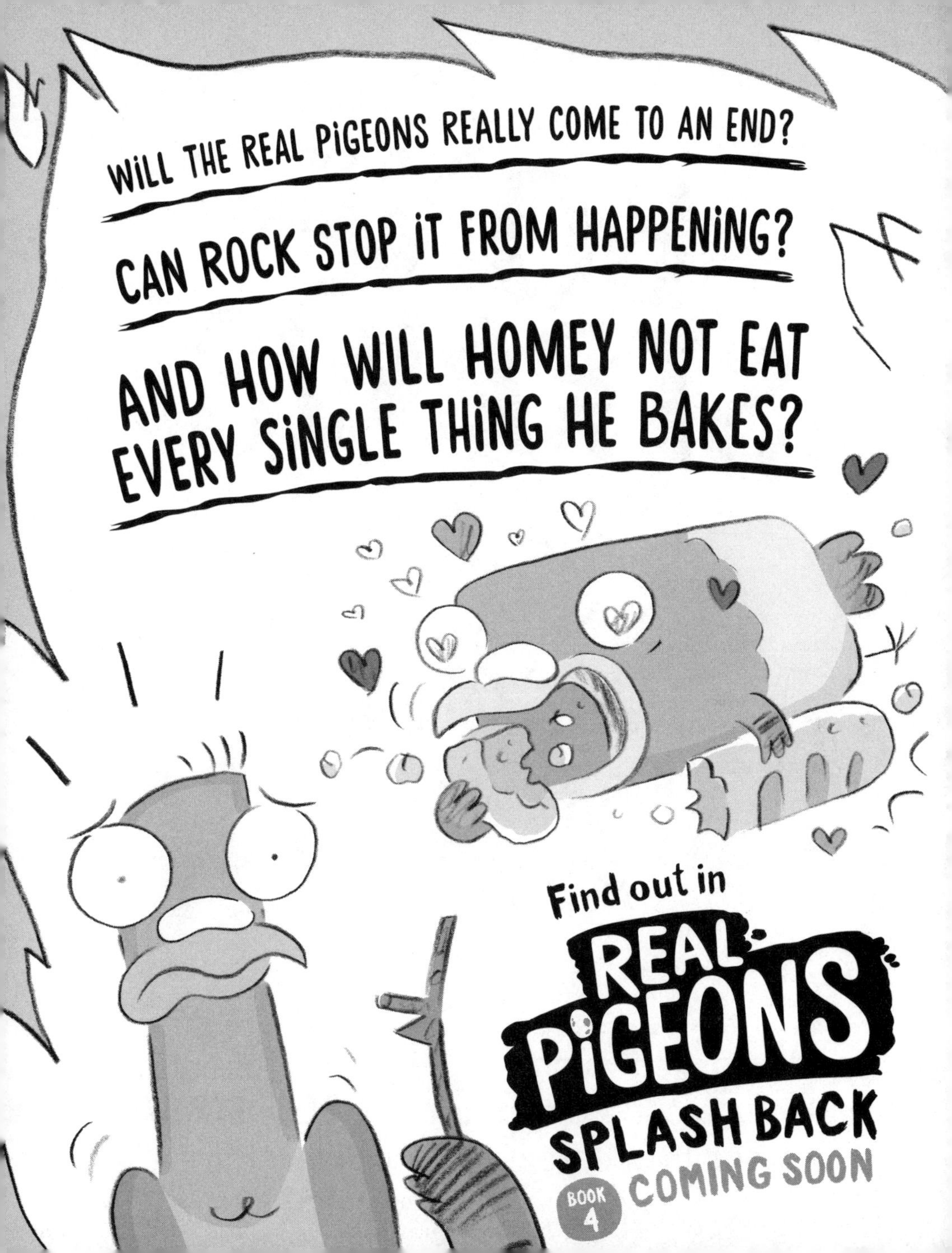
WILL THE REAL PIGEONS REALLY COME TO AN END?
CAN ROCK STOP IT FROM HAPPENING?
AND HOW WILL HOMEY NOT EAT EVERY SINGLE THING HE BAKES?
Find out in
REAL PIGEONS SPLASH BACK
COMING SOON
BOOK 4

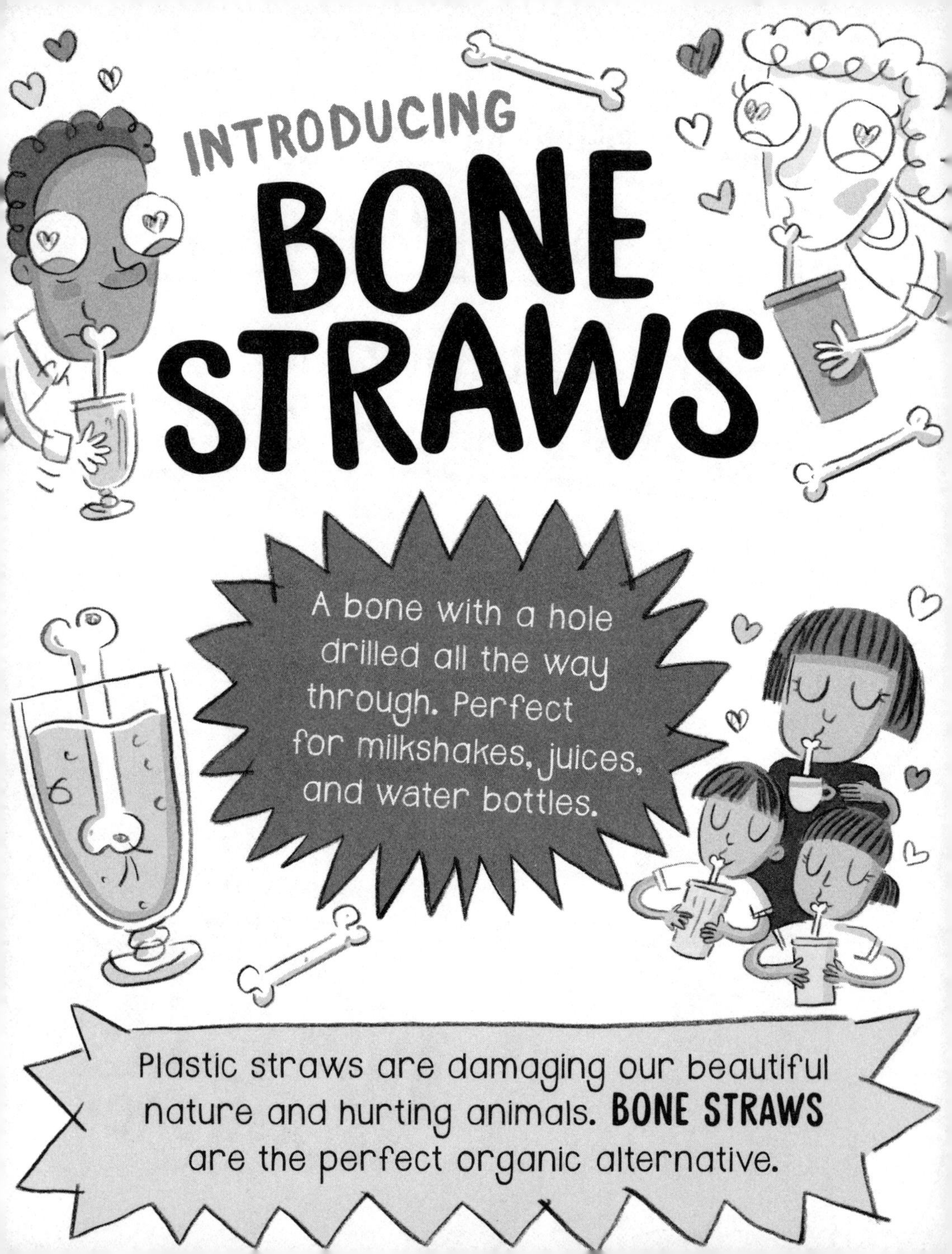

INTRODUCING
BONE STRAWS
A bone with a hole drilled all the way through. Perfect for milkshakes, juices, and water bottles.
Plastic straws are damaging our beautiful nature and hurting animals. BONE STRAWS are the perfect organic alternative.

"The best thing about using a **BONE STRAW** is that you can eat the **BONE** when you're done drinking!"

—B. Vulture

"Use a **BONE STRAW** next time you order a shake. And don't think too much about where the bone came from in the first place."

—L. Twitcher

#BONESTRAWS

MEET THE
TEAM

ANDREW
McDONALD
funny
author

BEN
WOOD
awesome
illustrator

ANDREW McDONALD is a writer from Melbourne, Australia. He lives with a lovely lady and a bouncy son and enjoys baking his own bread (which he eats down to the last bread crumb—sorry, pigeons!). Visit Andrew at mrandrewmcdonald.com.

BEN WOOD has illustrated more than twenty-five books for children. When Ben isn't drawing, he likes to eat food! His favorite foods include overstuffed burritos, green spaghetti, and big bags of chips! Yum! Visit Ben at benwood.com.au.

FIND OUT MORE ABOUT THE REAL PIGEONS SQUAD AT **REALPIGEONS.COM!**

DID YOU KNOW

REAL PIGEONS

ARE
REAL-LIFE
PIGEONS ?

ROCK PIGEON

The most common pigeon in the world. Gray with two black stripes on each wing. Very good at blending in!

FRILLBACK PIGEON

Known as a "fancy pigeon." Humans have bred them to be covered in curly feathers. These birds don't need to use hair curlers!

HOMING PIGEON

Has the incredible ability to fly long distances and return home from very far away. They were used to deliver letters many years ago.

TUMBLER PIGEON

Known to tumble or somersault while in flight. They fly normally before unexpectedly doing aerial acrobatics.

POUTER PIGEON

The big bubble that looks like a chest is actually called a crop. Pouters store food in their crops before releasing it to their stomachs. Yuck!

FIND OUT MORE AT REALPIGEONS.COM!

BEARDY VULTURE

Bearded vultures are very dramatic birds. They live high up in mountain crags. Their eyes are yellow with a circle of red around the edges. And they live on a diet of mostly bones. CRUNCH!

MORE REAL-LIFE CREATURES!

KID X

Kid X is a human child. Humans are a little bit like large, featherless pigeons who have mouths and teeth instead of beaks. They enjoy running around—but they need a hug from time to time.

JACKIE PIGEON

Jackie is a Jacobin pigeon—another kind of fancy pigeon. With their beautiful plumage and high, feathery collars, these pigeons look like rich celebrities. But no matter what they say, they are NOT royalty.

JUNGLE CROW

A bird with an incredibly large beak, a jungle crow is big and bossy in real life too! This crow will go to any length for a snack. He is also quite rude.

STRAW-NECK IBIS

Ibises used to hang out only in wetlands, but they've learned to live in cities too, where they enjoy eating out of trash cans. They look like small leftover dinosaurs, but they're actually pretty smart!

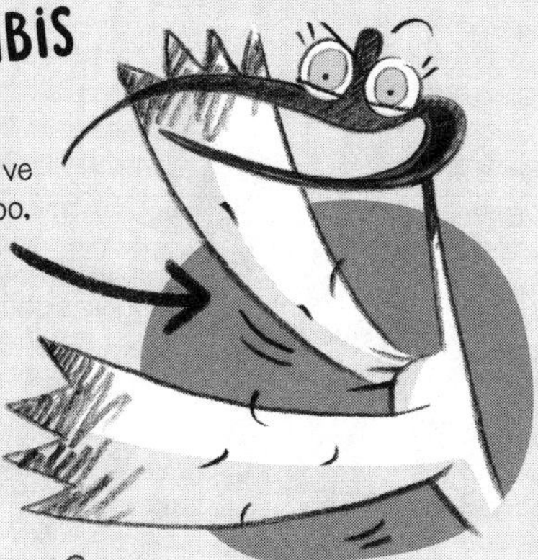

PEACOCK

Peacock is actually just the name for a male peafowl. Females are called peahens, and babies are called peachicks (cute!). An average adult peacock has over two hundred tail feathers with spots on each one. That's a lot of fake eyes!

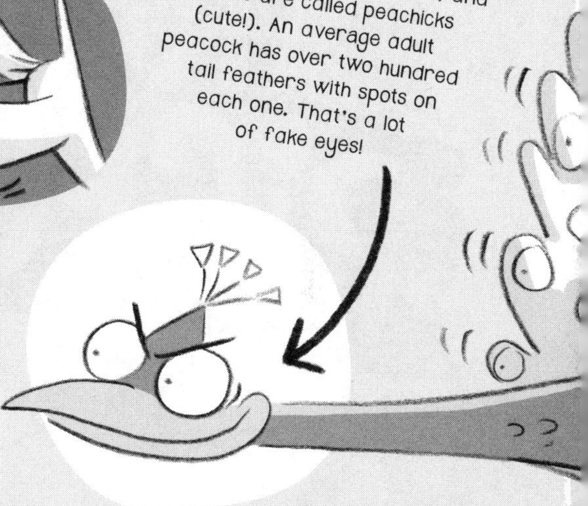

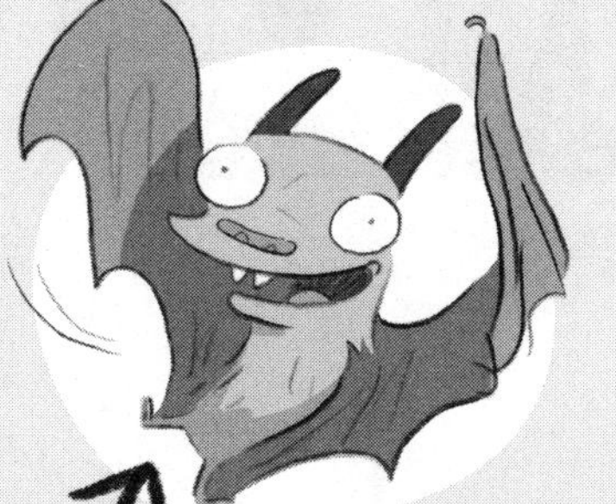

MEGABAT

Megabats are great at smelling things—that's how they locate fruit at night when they gather for dinner parties in fruit trees. True to their name, some megabats are really big, with a wingspan of up to 5.5 feet. Now that's mega!

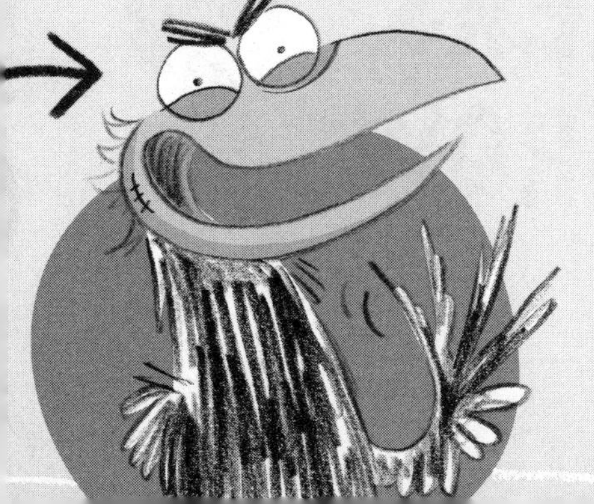

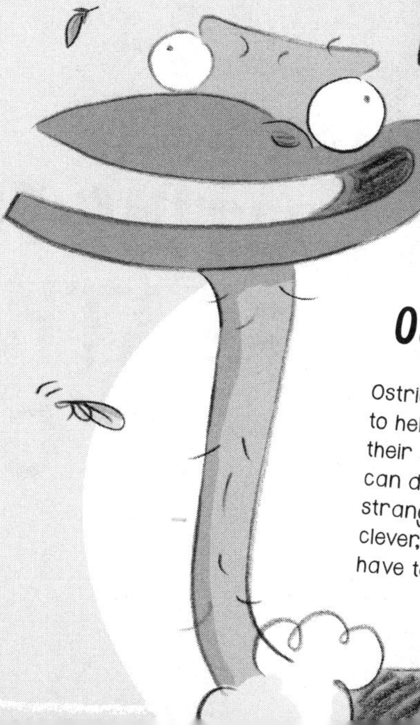

STRUTHIO OSTRICH

Ostriches swallow rocks to help break up food in their stomachs so that they can digest correctly. It's strange, but also pretty clever, since they don't have teeth!

REAL PIGEONS

FIGHT CRIME

1

ANDREW McDONALD · BEN WOOD

Join Rock and the squad as they solve mysterious mysteries like:

WHY HAVE ALL THE BREAD CRUMBS DISAPPEARED?

WHO IS KIDNAPPING BATS?

AND CAN THE REAL PIGEONS AVOID A DINNER DISASTER??

Join Rock and the squad as they solve
EVEN MORE mysterious mysteries like:

WHO IS TRAPPING BIRDS IN BOTTLES?

WHY IS THERE A DANGEROUS OSTRICH ON THE LOOSE?

CAN A FOOD FIGHT STOP AN EVIL PIE MAKER?

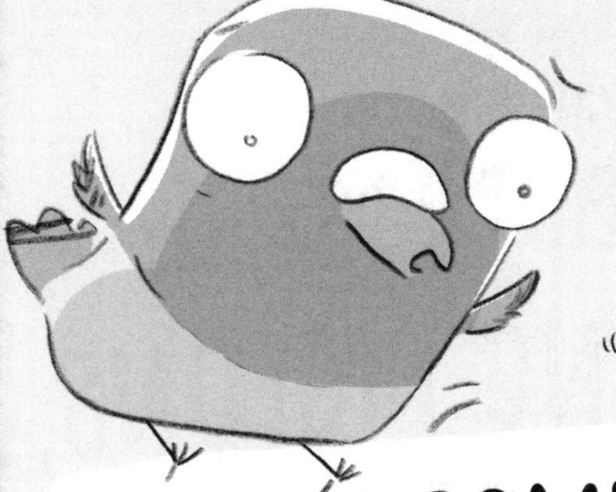

REAL PIGEONS
SPLASH BACK

BOOK 4 COMING SOON!

WHY HAS ALL THE WATER IN THE CITY VANISHED?

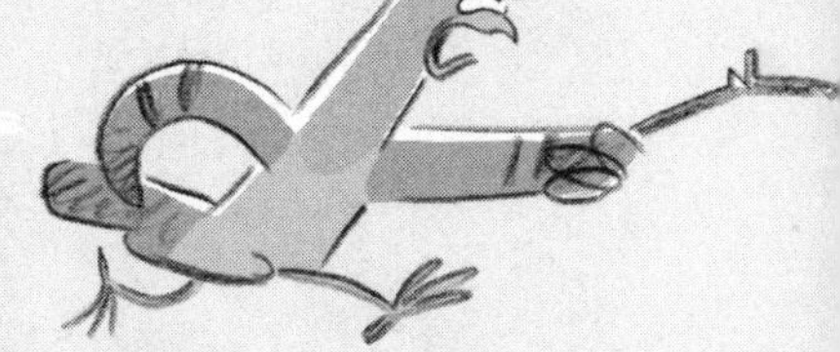

WHO IS THE SEASIDE PRANKSTER?

AND CAN THE REAL PIGEONS SAVE THE DAY . . .

AND THEMSELVES?

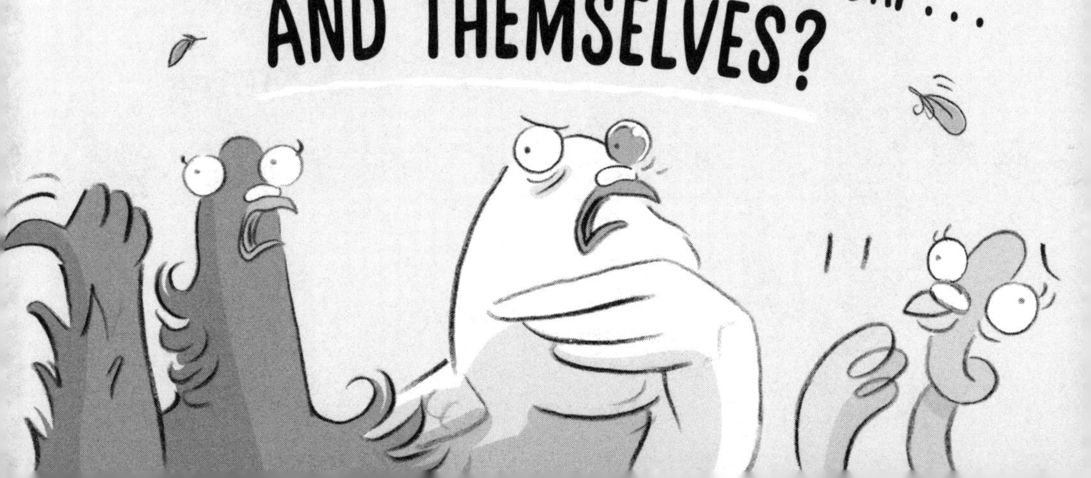

WHETHER YOU'RE LOOKING FOR KID ALIENS, ROBOT DOGS, OR CRIME-FIGHTING PIGEONS, WE'VE GOT THE SERIES FOR YOU!